ON
BLOOD
ROAD

STEVE WATKINS

ON BLOOD ROAD

Scholastic Press / New York

Library of Congress Cataloging-in-Publication Data available

ISBN 978-1-338-19701-3

10 9 8 7 6 5 4 3 2 1   18 19 20 21 22

Printed in the U.S.A.   23

First edition, November 2018

Book design by Nina Goffi

For Janet

January 22

My mom is waiting up when I come in—so late after midnight that I don't even bother looking at my watch. Our apartment is on the Upper West Side, on the nineteenth floor with a view of Central Park. Mom sleeps with earplugs and an eye mask, and her bedroom is a mile away from the elevator, so I don't know how she heard me.

But here she is, her usually perfect hair all frizzy, no makeup, standing right inside the front door with her arms crossed, tapping her foot. The ash on her cigarette is so long I think it will fall onto the plush carpet that she just had installed. Like she's been waiting for me for who knows how long. The whole scene catches me off guard.

"Where have you been?" she demands, as I peel off my coat and scarf and this Russian winter army hat with fur-lined flaps that I wear all the time. "And don't even think about lying to me, Taylor, because I will find out. I will call every one of your friends' parents, and be assured that someone will know something."

I spent the past few hours at a music club called Max's Kansas City with my best friend, Geoff, and two girls from our French class, and a couple hundred other people, all of us packed in so tight that nobody could dance, just sway in rhythm. A psychedelic West Coast band called Moby Grape had been playing.

"Concert," I say. "In the Village. So what?"

Mom looks for an ashtray, finds one, stubs out her cigarette, and glares at me.

"Don't you 'So what' me, young man. You know you're not allowed out at night without permission and an escort. We are in New York City. You could be hurt, or mugged, or killed. And it's a school night!"

I know I should just apologize and get it over with and blah, blah, blah. But since when did she start caring what I do? I feel a flare of resentment at this sudden show of concern. Normally I'm invisible while she's off planning charity events and silent auctions and whatever else she does as an excuse to dress up and hang out with other rich moms and brag about their lives.

"Isn't it kind of late for you to be up?" I retort. "Isn't this, like, when you get your beauty sleep? Put cold cream all over your face? Talk to Dad?"

My dad is a Special Attaché for Something or Other at the US embassy—in Vietnam of all places, which is why when he calls it's at all kinds of weird hours. He isn't home much. Too busy working on the war, or pumping up the South Vietnamese economy, or making his own business deals on the side, or whatever. It's 1968, and President Johnson keeps assuring us that we're winning the war, that there's light at the end of the tunnel, that the American troops—half a million and counting—will be home soon from Southeast Asia. It's all over the nightly news.

"As a matter of fact, I already spoke with your father," Mom snaps. "And when he wanted to talk to you and you had snuck out, well, that was it. He agrees with me that you have been out of control lately, and it's time we did something about it."

Wanted to talk to me? Yeah, right. Ever since my dad left for Vietnam, I haven't exactly been of high interest to him. More like my mom asked if he wanted to talk to me and he felt obligated to say yes.

"Did something like what?" I ask, but then I interrupt her before she can even get started. "You know what? Never mind. You can tell me in the morning. I'm tired. I'm going to bed. Got school tomorrow, remember?"

I try to step past her, but she blocks me. "Oh no you don't," she says. "You're going to hear me out. This isn't the first time your so-called friends have talked you into sneaking out of the apartment and going to hippie clubs in the Village. Especially that boy Geoffrey you're always hanging out with."

I throw myself down on the sofa, resigning myself to whatever she wants to say. "How do you know I'm not the one who's the bad influence on Geoff? Huh? Ever thought about that?"

Mom's face turns beet red, but she plows on, listing ways I'm the worst kid. "Your grades are atrocious. You're barely passing classes and you're on academic probation. I don't understand what your problem is. Do you know how many kids would kill to go to the Dalton School?"

I brush my hair out of my face and shrug at her.

"And your hair! You look homeless with it that long." She seems like she's picking up steam, so I tune out, until she says, "We're taking you out of school. For the next two weeks. Whether we send you back will depend on how you conduct yourself during that time."

I laugh. "Sweet! A vacation. And we just had Christmas break!"

"You'll be accompanying me to visit your father for his fiftieth birthday, which is next week if you forgot," she says.

"No way!" I shout. "Did *you* forget he's in Vietnam, and there's a little something called a war going on over there?"

"The war is in the North," Mom says. "In the Central Highlands. Your father explained it all to me. There is guerrilla activity in the South, but it is contained. Most of it was eradicated in military operations last year. So we'll be safe."

4

I roll my eyes. She sounds like she's reading one of Dad's secret briefing papers that he sometimes forgets are supposed to be so secret. He had a stack of them with him when he came home for a week at Christmas. He was so busy poring over his precious documents and talking on the phone and making day trips down to Washington that I barely got to see him. I thought I'd finally get to hang out with him, but guess I'm the idiot. Good thing Geoff found plenty of stuff for us to do.

I can't believe this is happening. One minute I'm grooving with Geoff and some girls to Moby Grape, and now this? One of the girls, Beth, just started at our school. Geoff and the other girl, Cassandra, hooked me up with her when we met in the Village. And so far, so good. Beth is sixteen like me, and pretty, with straight brown hair that's so long she can practically sit on it. She and I stuck together the whole night, dancing, or I guess swaying, at Max's. When we all split up afterward, Beth gave me a flower she'd been wearing behind her ear and said we should hang out again sometime.

"Well, I'm not going," I announce to my mom, sounding like a little kid. "And you can't make me."

She smiles for the first time—an icy smile that makes her look less like her usual Hollywood star and more like Cruella de Vil. "We'll see about that," she says. "You are a minor, and as a minor, you don't get to make these decisions for yourself."

"I'll run away," I say, knowing I sound even more childish.

"You'll do what you're told," she says, and that's the end of it.

A week later, on a stone-cold January afternoon, Mom and I take off on a Continental Airlines flight to Saigon—twenty hours sitting side by side, not saying a word, at least not to each other. It's been a long week of silence in our apartment. We're in first class so she can talk to the other rich people, and I can stretch out with my portable eight-track tape player and headphones and a new album by the Doors. I listen to the song "Love Me Two Times" over and over, thinking about Beth. We talked on the phone a couple of times since that night at Max's Kansas City. When I told her my mom was making me go to Vietnam, she went all Romeo and Juliet about it. She made me promise I wouldn't get killed, as if she thought I was going into the army instead of just getting dragged away for two weeks to visit my dad.

I told Geoff and he laughed his butt off. "Dude, you get to go to Vietnam, the coolest, most wretched place on the planet. What do you care about some girl? Two weeks of exotic vacation in beautiful, bombed-out Southeast Asia. Wish I could get punished like that."

"They might not let me come back to school," I said.

"Big deal," he said. "You're gonna get drafted anyway when

you turn eighteen. Unless you do like I'm planning and go the conscientious objector route."

Geoff had dragged me to this big antiwar demonstration last year, a hundred thousand people marching from Central Park to the United Nations in an April downpour, demanding an end to the war, burning draft cards, singing Bob Dylan songs. Martin Luther King Jr. was one of the leaders. Him and the baby doctor, Benjamin Spock.

"My dad's head will explode if I don't register for the draft," I said. "Better yet, he thinks I should enlist like he did in World War II. And like his dad in World War I. I thought he was going to fly home and strangle me when Mom told him about the protest march."

"Yeah, I remember that," Geoff said. "Too bad you and your dad can't just, you know, sit down and talk about it. Half the country wants us out of Vietnam already."

"Hey, what can I tell you?" I said. "War is the family business."

January 28

Heat waves rise like wobbly spirits off the black tarmac on the runway at Tan Son Nhat Airport outside Saigon. We flew inland about forty miles from the South China Sea, following the Saigon River—the pilot pointed out all the various landmarks—and now we're here. But from the looks of things outside the air-conditioned airliner, I'm not sure I want to get off the plane.

Sure enough, as soon as we step out onto the asphalt, the heat slams into me like I walked into a wall. I'm drenched in sweat by the time we trudge over to the terminal, though Mom seems oblivious. She's gotten dolled up in a pink dress, but it turns out Dad isn't here to meet us. He sent his car and driver, a middle-aged Vietnamese guy named Hanh, followed by a jeep with a couple of marines, one of them sitting in the back behind a mounted machine gun.

"Are we gonna need that?" I ask Hanh, surprised to see such a heavily armed escort. I thought Saigon was supposed to be safe. "Do we have to, like, fight our way to the embassy?"

"It is only a precaution," Hanh says, holding the door open for Mom. She stops to stare at the machine gun, too, obviously not pleased.

The AC is cranked up as high as it will go in the car, a new Ford sedan that Hanh assures us is armor-plated and has bulletproof windows.

"I guess those are only a precaution, too?" I say.

"Yes," Hanh says. "Saigon is well protected. But all of the country is a war zone."

The shock back into AC from the one-hundred-degree heat gives me a headache. I press my hands against my temples and wish I'd gotten that haircut Mom has been on me about, since my long hair is now damp with humidity and matted to my forehead and the back of my neck. I think I might have to grab it and twist to ring out all the water.

Mom, who never seems to sweat no matter what, coolly adjusts her Foster Grant sunglasses and waits like royalty while Hanh retrieves our luggage. Then we're off to find Dad's villa, which is near the embassy in the center of Saigon on a street called Thong Nhut Boulevard. We only know the names because Hanh keeps up a running commentary from the front seat like one of those New York tour bus operators.

Mom nods politely for a while, then orders him to stop at a

stand to buy us cold Coca-Colas. "And be sure they haven't already been opened," she admonishes him.

"Of course," he says.

To me she adds, "Whatever you do, be sure not to drink the water unless it's been boiled."

We pass through a blur of streets and highways, some so wide they look like parking lots, others so narrow you can almost reach out and push over the tin-roofed houses and stores crowding the edges. There are old, boxy 1950s cars, most of them taxis, fighting their way through intersections and around traffic circles with no signals or police to direct things. That means bicycles and pedestrians and rickshaws and scooters and even horses and wagons are all thrown together in a crazy swirling chaos as one traffic jam bleeds into the next, with just the occasional open block where Hanh can shift into second gear.

There are kids everywhere, running in and out of traffic, squatting in alleys, standing like zombies, splashing in puddles, or begging for piastres just inches from our window as we nudge our way through—some dressed in rags, some with shirts but no pants, some with nothing on at all.

Mom tells me not to give them anything. "It will only encourage them to be bolder," she says. I'm used to seeing panhandlers in New York, but these are just kids.

Helicopters flash above us, swooping low over the city. "American," Hanh says. "Routine patrols."

We pass a Ford dealership that only has junked cars and rusty car parts, splash through open sewers, see a pit filled with chemical-brown water and dozens of kids swimming in it. There are tarpaulin-covered stalls with cases of bottled sodas stacked ten feet high. Women crouching on sidewalks cooking on tiny stoves. More kids sitting on blankets or towels or just sitting in the dirt selling pyramids of Pall Mall cigarettes and cans of sardines. A giant billboard for a Jerry Lewis movie with a rendering of the comedian that makes him look demonic. Women in long dresses with slits on the side that Hanh tells us are called ao dai. Girls in Western miniskirts and halter tops and high heels and heavy makeup. Hanh catches me staring.

"Those are B-Girls," he says to my mother. "It is best for the young man to stay away from them."

"Thank you," Mom says, throwing a warning glance at me, but I keep looking at the girls.

After an hour, we enter the old French business district at the center of Saigon—or so Hanh tells us—where the streets all widen again, shaded by towering tamarind trees and lined with bougainvillea and fire-red poinciana. We pass the Hotel Continental, which Hanh says is the oldest hotel in Saigon. "Built by the French so of course it's very fancy."

What isn't so fancy is the wall of sandbags blocking the entrance, and more sandbags protecting other government-looking buildings. The architecture changes here. Red-tile roofs, shining white columns. Most of the people we see now are Vietnamese businessmen in dress pants and long-sleeved white shirts, and an increasing number of South Vietnamese Army types and American GIs.

"For many years, until France gave up Vietnam as a colony, Saigon was called the Paris of the East," Hanh the Tour Guide says as the Continental and its wall of sandbags disappear behind us.

Mom asks about shopping and Hanh points out several stores as we pass that he must think are upscale, but judging from the sour expression on her face, my mom doesn't agree.

We pass a small forest of dinosaur-size trees, with trunks growing out of trunks growing out of trunks, and branches rising higher than the surrounding buildings, easily over five stories tall, with monkeys and birds crowding the upper reaches and small shrines decorating the ground underneath.

"Banyan trees," Hanh says. "They are a species of fig trees. The figs attract the monkeys and birds and fruit bats you see in the branches."

"What's with the shrines?" I ask.

"Those are for ancestor worship," Hanh says. "Many of the people in South Vietnam follow the Catholic religion, but there are still many Buddhists as well. The Buddhists believe spirits live in banyan trees, so during Tet they leave gifts and sacrifices and say prayers for their ancestors."

"What is Tet?" Mom asks. "Is that a local celebration of some kind?"

Hanh laughs. "Not exactly. Tet is the Vietnamese New Year, which begins in two days, just after midnight. This coming year will be the Year of the Monkey."

He doesn't have time to explain further, because we're suddenly there, pulling into Dad's gated villa, a compound with shards of glass embedded in the top of a concrete wall, and a roll of concertina wire behind that—plus a guard house with two armed, scowling Vietnamese soldiers with M16s. The villa itself is two stories, with a veranda running all the way around the second floor. Dad's basically turned his house into a heavily defended bunker. The Germans he fought in World War II would have loved the place.

Hanh parks in a circular driveway under tall tamarind trees and ushers us inside. The military jeep with the machine gun stays out on the street. The burst of heat between the car and the villa is a little easier to deal with thanks to the shade, but the humidity is still so thick a machete would come in handy.

Dad isn't home. "I'm very sorry," Hanh says. "It appears Ambassador Sorenson is still at work."

"He's an ambassador now?" I ask. "When did he get a promotion?"

"It's just an honorary title, Taylor," my mom says as she opens her purse. Hanh smiles and nods.

Mother tries to tip him, but he waves her off. "Though perhaps you will want to leave a gratuity for the staff when you depart," he says. He sets our suitcases down in the foyer, then summons the housekeeper, the gardener, the cook, and their assistants, so he can introduce them to us and explain their duties. They all nod but mostly look at the floor. None speak.

"Welcome to Saigon," Hanh says after the introductions and the help have retreated to their stations or duties or whatever. "Let me know if you need anything."

"It would be nice to have my dad here to at least greet us," I say. "Maybe you can give him the message?"

"Enough with the sarcasm," Mom says. "I'm sure your father is very busy."

"He's always very busy," I say.

Hanh just keeps smiling.

Dad and I get into it about the war half an hour after he shows up at the villa that night—so late that Mom has long since gone to bed. She must be too jet-lagged and out of it to rouse herself when he pulls up with a convoy of military escort vehicles that goes zooming away into the Saigon night once he's inside. He barely says a word to me, just pours himself a nightcap and announces that we're going to have ourselves a little talk, man to man. Since we just saw each other in New York the month before over Christmas, I guess he figures he can skip the part where the absent parent tells his kid how much he missed him and just get right to the lecturing.

With no choice, I follow Dad into his study, which is a mess of papers and files and books and magazines and documents and a desk buried under there somewhere. A ceiling fan turns in slow motion, hardly moving the stagnant air. He kicks back in a recliner. I'm left with a straight-back chair against the wall.

"Your mother tells me you've been sneaking out, going to clubs, thinking you're some kind of hotshot," he says, pulling a cigar out of a silver box on a lamp stand next to his chair. He rolls the cigar between his fingers, sniffs it, then clips off the end. He fires up the cigar and lets out a stream of smoke. I cough for what seems like five minutes and feel dizzy afterward. He tilts his head back and blows smoke rings up at the ceiling fan.

"So what about it, hotshot?" he asks. "Got anything to say for yourself?"

"What's there to say?" I respond. "Mom already pulled me out of school. Said you guys might not send me back. That's about it."

I think he'll get angry about me being so flip, but he lets it go. Just keeps blowing those smoke rings, some of which manage to shoot between the fan blades. He sips his drink, looks at it, then downs the rest in one gulp.

"So how about the war, Dad?" I say, angry that he doesn't even seem to care enough to respond. "How's that going lately? You got this thing won yet? Just about ready to wrap things up? Turn off the light at the end of the tunnel and send everybody home?"

Dad fixes his gaze on me and holds it there, jaw clenched, until I look away, already regretting the sarcasm. Why do I have to be such an idiot all the time? Most people are afraid of my dad— because of his size and his temper, and because he's always right and wants to make sure everybody knows it.

He crosses one leg over the other, stubs out the cigar on the bottom of his shoe, lets the ashes drop on the floor.

Then he proceeds to lecture me for the next hour, until past midnight, pausing only long enough to refill his glass. Tonight's inspiring Frank Sorenson lecture covers everything: the dangers of international communism, the brutality and depravity of the North Vietnamese who love nothing better than to torture and maim, the soulless assassinations of innocent village leaders by the Viet Cong guerrilla fighters, the gutless hippies and traitorous peaceniks back in the States who are undermining support for the troops, the ungrateful punks like me who have everything handed to them on a silver platter and take for granted the free-doms and prosperity as Americans that people like him spend their lives defending and insuring will continue by taking on—and taking out—the dark forces in the world that those same ungrateful punks can't even begin to imagine exist, but that are all too real.

By that point, he's really on a roll, and, driving his lecture home, he says he just wishes he could send me out into the field for a day with an army patrol on a search and destroy mission, because then I'd know what real fear is, and real courage, and true patriot-ism, and understand that in the real world—the world he lives in and that I do, too, I just don't know it yet (but one day I am sure going to find out)—it comes down to just this: kill or be killed.

He stops and looks at me expectantly, like, *Well? What have you got to say for yourself now?*

It's been an impressive verbal vomit, that's for sure. But I have nothing, and even if I did, what's the point?

So instead I just say, "Happy birthday, Dad," which isn't much of a comeback—isn't a comeback at all—but at least it's true.

January 29

Khe Sanh, Khe Sanh, Khe Sanh. That's all anybody is talking about at the embassy the next day when Mom and I go in at noon so Dad can show us around. It's officially his fiftieth birthday, not that he seems to care, as distracted as he is by the latest developments in the war. He tells us the North Vietnamese Army—Dad just calls them the NVA—has surrounded a US Marine base at a place called Khe Sanh in the demilitarized zone between North and South Vietnam. That was a week ago, but the marines still haven't been able to break the siege. And there are indications that there might be more coordinated attacks by the NVA and their guerrilla units—the Viet Cong—on some major cities and other military bases north of Saigon. Dad's clearly concerned, but at the same time kind of excited. Not like he's giddy and clapping his hands and stuff, but it's obvious that his adrenaline is pumping since he can't sit still and jumps every time his phone rings.

When he sees the worried look on Mom's face, though, he goes into protector mode and assures her that Saigon is hundreds of miles south of all that business and crawling with US and South Vietnamese military, so he doesn't see that there's anything to worry about down where we are. She smiles and kisses him, then says, "I'm sure you can handle whatever comes up."

What I think is: So much for the light at the end of the tunnel. If the North Vietnamese Army can lay siege to a thousand marines in their heavily fortified camp, trap them there, and attack cities around South Vietnam, it sure doesn't sound like the war is wrapping up any time soon, no matter what President Johnson— and my dad—have to say about it.

Dad takes us out to dinner that night at what's supposed to be a fancy Vietnamese restaurant, but it's a disaster—at least it is for Mom, who freaks out about the food. I think it's cool—stuff like tripe, which is, like, the stomach lining of a cow, and fish eyeballs, which Dad says are supposed to be a delicacy, and squid teeth.

"Isn't there someplace else we can go?" Mom says. She avoids even looking at the food. "A nice French restaurant?"

I'm chewing on a mouthful of fried frog, which is rubbery and kind of tastes like chicken. Dad winks at me, and for a minute it's like old times with him and me, like partners in crime, co-conspirators. I make a big show of trying everything—the tripe, the eyeballs, even the squid teeth. Dad actually says, "That's my boy."

Mom asks for coffee, but when they bring it out, Dad stops her. "You might not want to drink that," he says. "It's not what you think."

Mom dips her spoon in the black liquid and lifts it out, as if she expects to find something disgusting floating around in there. "What is it?" she asks.

Dad laughs. It's the first time I've heard him do that since I can't even remember when. "It's weasel dung coffee," he says. "They feed coffee beans to weasels. The beans come out partly digested, but with a distinctive flavor. It's an acquired taste."

I laugh so hard it makes me spit out an eyeball, which only makes me laugh even harder.

Mom storms out of the restaurant. Dad shrugs and says, "Better follow her," and off we go. I'm secretly glad to get away from all the food—it was getting to be a bit much—and relieved when we end up in a French restaurant at the Hotel Continental. But the mood changes there. From the minute we step inside, Dad quits being the Dad he was when it was me and him versus Mom at the Vietnamese place, and turns back into his war self—nodding to a table full of generals, who invite us to join them, stopping to talk to more tables full of men in suits, holding court through dinner as a steady stream of people make their way over to our table to talk shop. He eventually disappears into the bar, saying he'll be right back. He's gone for the rest of dinner.

Mom and I finish eating alone. She doesn't speak to me, just sits there fuming, and she won't speak to Dad, either, when he finally comes back, except to shove his birthday present at him. "Here," she says, as we're leaving the restaurant. "It's a tie."

I forgot to get him a gift and tell myself he doesn't deserve anything anyway.

━━━━━━━━━━━━━━━━

I spend the next day with Hanh checking out Saigon, though he's under strict orders from Mom not to let me out of his sight and to make sure we're back in time for this big formal embassy dinner that evening to celebrate the first night of Tet. He might be under strict orders not to say much about the war, too, judging by the non-answers he gives when I ask him about it. I do find out that he was a captain in the South Vietnamese Army—the ARVN— and assigned to the American embassy. He learned English at the Defense Language Institute in California, where he lived when he was sent there for three months and served as a transla- tor for American officers in the field interrogating NVA prisoners and suspected spies.

"So why drive a car for my father?" I ask. "And why no uniform?"

"I am your father's personal translator when he goes into the field," Hanh says. "For that, I have the highest security clearance. I offered to also serve as his driver so I could be close by whenever

I am needed. It was decided that I should wear street clothes on the job to be less of a target," he added. "The Viet Cong may be anywhere, even in Saigon. If I appear to be nothing more than a hired driver, with an American businessman, it will be safer."

"What about the military escort we had yesterday?" I ask. "And last night when we went out to dinner?"

Hanh had waited in the car while we were in the two restaurants. I noticed Dad didn't bother to invite him to join us.

He shrugs. "Only sometimes." He gestures behind us. "No one is with us now, as you can see."

Hanh pretty much keeps to the tourist spots on our tour of the city—Saigon City Hall, back by the Hotel Continental, through the Saigon market, though he won't let me get out of the car because he says he's worried about pickpockets. He takes me by the Saigon Opera House of all places and the Notre Dame Cathedral. We could be in the real Paris, where we lived when I was a little kid, except for all the Vietnamese people walking in the streets. Hanh drives us to the ancient palace where the old Vietnamese emperors used to live, and then to the Saigon Zoo. He must think I'm in elementary school. The only cool thing at the pathetic zoo is more banyan trees. I climb one way above Hanh and everybody else, except for some kids who see me and climb that high, too. And, of course, there are the monkeys, who chatter wildly, as if they own the place and want us to leave already, because they're not about to share any of their figs. I'm dripping with sweat but happy being up in the banyan tree. I think about that girl Beth and how cool it would be to climb up here with her.

Geoff would love being here, too. Though knowing him, he'd bring water balloons for us to throw at people walking past down on the ground. Which probably wouldn't be such a good idea in Saigon. There's a lot of military around here that looks a little trigger-happy.

If Geoff were here, we'd be out turning Saigon upside down already. He wouldn't be stuck like I am, being babysat by my dad's driver. Ever since Geoff and I met at Dalton—the slowest guys in the slowest lane on the swim team—he's been getting me into the kinds of trouble that make life a lot more interesting than following the rules. "It doesn't matter what happens," he's always saying. "As long as you get a good story out of it."

When I climb down, Hanh is talking to another Vietnamese man. The man leaves as soon as he sees me, disappearing down a dusty path and into a thicket of thirsty bougainvillea.

"Who was that?" I ask.

"Just a friend."

He doesn't say anything more, but it doesn't matter. I'm just being polite. What I really want to know is where somebody might go in Saigon if they want to kick off the Vietnamese New Year right. A club or something. It's the sort of thing Geoff would have already found out and come up with a plan for sneaking off and getting there.

Hanh shakes his head. "It isn't safe to venture into Saigon at night without an escort," he says.

"Oh sure, of course not," I say. "I was just wondering."

Hanh hesitates, then says, "There's always a big Tet celebration in Cholon, the Chinese section of town, down next to the Saigon River. Music halls and fireworks and street parties." He taps his chin and smiles, adding, "Bunny Bunny Go Go is a dance club with strobe lights and B-Girls and Vietnamese bands playing covers of American Top Forty. Very popular with Western visitors. But of course you are much too young."

"Yeah, of course," I say, thinking that sounds a lot more interesting—and will make for a much better story—than sticking around for my dad's work party.

⸺⸺⸺⸺⸺

I manage to cut out of the embassy party that night around eleven, though it's still going strong—or at least strong in a boring, fancy dress, diplomatic sort of way. "Sayonara, suckers," I mutter as I slip out a side door. I doubt Mom will notice. She's been busy all night establishing herself as the queen of embassy society, flaunting her furs and pearls, doing the Jackie Kennedy thing with a pillbox hat and elbow-length gloves. She probably wishes she could trade in the hat for a tiara. Dad, meanwhile, has positioned himself in a back corner of the room, where a steady stream of diplomats in tuxedos and generals in their dress uniforms keep sidling up to him and holding whispered conversations, kind of like the night before at the French restaurant. It's like the real ambassador, Ellsworth Bunker, is the master of ceremonies, but Special Attaché Frank Sorenson is one of those old mafia dons, the dark figure in the shadows with all the real power, the one who is running the show.

I have big plans with a girl named Cindy I met earlier that evening. Her parents also pulled her out of school somewhere else back in the States. She says she's been bored since they got to Vietnam and is up for anything. We sat next to each other during dinner, danced a couple of times to the corny big band playing old-people music. She kept putting her hand on my arm and leaving it there, like we were already a couple or something.

As soon as we get outside she does even more than that, pulling me close and kissing me. She apparently thinks I'm cool because I'm from New York, and I'm more than happy to let her think that.

We make out for a few minutes, until she gently pushes me away. "Wow," she says. "You're a good kisser."

I doubt it—I haven't had a lot of practice—but I say, "You too," anyway.

"So I was thinking," Cindy says. "Instead of going out, why don't we stay here and get to know each other, you know, better?" She presses her lips together. "And we can do *that* some more, too."

"You're chickening out?" I say. "I thought we were going to hit the town? You said you wanted to go."

"Yeah," she says. "About that. I don't know. It seemed like a good idea, but look around." She gestures to the dark night sky that surrounds us, everything disappearing into the shadows. "And my dad said they were attacking cities and stuff. So it's possible they could even attack here . . ." She trails off.

"Girls in New York wouldn't chicken out," I say, annoyed that she's bailing because I don't really want to go alone.

She looks down, embarrassed.

"Fine," I say. "Whatever. Stay here if you want. But I'm taking off." I turn to leave.

"You really shouldn't," she says. "Really. It's not safe."

I stop. A part of me wants to stay, and maybe fool around with Cindy in the bushes or wherever we can get a little privacy. There are embassy guards patrolling the grounds.

But when am I ever going to have an opportunity like this again—to sneak out at midnight in Vietnam? I can practically hear Geoff telling me I have to do it: *the coolest, most wretched place on Earth.*

"Catch you later," I say to Cindy, heading for the embassy gate.

It's almost midnight in Saigon. It's Tet. Let the Year of the Monkey begin.

Time to hit Bunny Bunny Go Go and party like there's no tomorrow.

January 30, almost midnight

The tuk-tuk driver is playing that singsong wailing they call pop music here, but as soon as I get in and tell him where I'm going, he switches channels on his little transistor radio to the armed forces station. It must be psychedelic hour because they're playing Jefferson Airplane, the Doors, the Rolling Stones. The closer we get to Cholon, the more congested the streets, with fireworks blasting, fires blazing in oil drums, people staggering around, stumbling into traffic, old men and women so stooped over from age they look like hunchbacks, street vendors selling everything from meat on sticks to guns. The night air is warm but still feels cooler than the crippling ninety-plus heat of daytime. I'm wearing this stupid black suit that Mom insisted I put on for the embassy dinner, with a wide paisley tie that she nearly died when she saw but that I refused to take off. I also have on a pair of Dad's wing tip shoes that are two sizes too big, but she said would have to do since I didn't bring any dress shoes of my own, and there was no way she was going to let me wear my Chuck Taylors or desert boots.

The tuk-tuk driver tries to make conversation in his broken English, asking if I'm a big American, whatever that means, and if I'm going out to party. He leers at me in his cracked rearview mirror. "Make big fun with Vietnam girls?"

"Sure," I say, trying to sound more confident than I feel. Earlier, I was all about breaking out and joining the party, impressing Geoff, but now that I'm on my own, heading for Cholon, nervousness sets in. What am I thinking? I can't be doing something like this. Sure, I snuck out in New York, but that was with Geoff. Never just me, alone. Like now, zipping past tin-roof shacks and concrete block houses with torn awnings and teetering high-rises that look like they're held up by matchsticks and mud. And wild chickens and scrawny dogs and bats and bugs so big they can probably carry off a small kid.

Before I can tell the driver to turn around and take me back to the embassy, though, we're deep inside Cholon, and whatever forward momentum has taken me this far pulls me out of the tuk-tuk and onto the crazy street in front of Bunny Bunny Go Go. I pay the driver a lot more than I should and he takes off, leaving me standing there looking ridiculous—and scared—in a cloud of exhaust.

I step toward the entrance, but that is as far as I get before somebody calls my name.

"Taylor Sorenson!"

I can't believe it. How can anybody know me here?

I turn to see a jeep with two US Army MPs—military police—pulling up behind me. "You Taylor Sorenson?"

I nod, still so shocked that I can't speak. People around us stop what they're doing to stand and stare—and point and laugh.

"You need to come with us," one of the MPs says.

"Why?" I ask. "How'd you know it was me?"

They laugh, too. "Apparently, somebody at the embassy got worried about you and sent out word that you were on your way here," he says. "We were dispatched to intercept."

His partner points his nightstick at me. "Yeah. You been busted."

I just stand there for a minute, defeated. Cindy must have ratted me out, mad because I abandoned her back at the embassy, and when word got back to Dad he notified the military police.

Music pulses out of the nightclub every time the doors swing open. A lot of loud guitar and earsplitting reverb and machine-gun percussion. A lot of smoke and shrieking and strobe lights.

I climb into the back of the jeep. I was already feeling stupid before in my black suit and loud tie and oversize shoes. Now I feel even stupider.

"Hey, don't worry about it, kid," the other MP says. "Look at it this way—not too many your age would have even made it this far. Plus I guarantee, you did not want to see what was on the other side of the doors to a place like that. People in there—they'll steal you blind before you even know they've got hold of your wallet. And you'll be lucky if that's all that happens to you."

"Yeah, think of it like we just did you a big favor, pal," the second MP says as he guns the jeep forward and away from the party.

We only make it a little way, though, maybe a hundred yards, before we run into a South Vietnamese Army patrol blocking traffic. Two soldiers with automatic weapons hanging off their shoulders wave us to a stop. The MPs curse, then get out of the jeep to see what's up. One of them says something to the ARVN soldiers in Vietnamese that sounds like he's reading from a phrasebook. I can feel a headache coming on.

I close my eyes and rub my temples, just for a second, slumping back in my seat, until a loud burst of fireworks right next to the jeep jolts me upright.

At first I can't see anything but smoke, with a strange, acrid smell that stings my nose. I break into a coughing fit until it clears.

Where are the MPs? Why are the ARVN soldiers waving their weapons at people on the street? Why is everybody cowering like that? There's a loud ringing in my ears. The fireworks must have been closer than I thought. I shake my head, lean forward in the jeep, see the MPs lying in the street, but can't figure out why they're doing that. Maybe they got scared by the fireworks, thought it was gunfire and dove for cover.

The ARVN soldiers are pointing their guns in my direction now. People on the street are running away. The soldiers are talking excitedly, gesturing my way, shaking their weapons, looking down at the MPs. I don't understand any of it—why the MPs *still* aren't moving, why they're just lying there like that. Why the soldiers are coming toward the jeep now, and yelling at me in their rapid-fire Vietnamese.

One of the soldiers waves his gun in a way that I finally understand means he wants me to get out of the jeep, which I do, moving as slowly and carefully as possible, still trying to make sense of what's going on. I step closer to the MPs and see a pool of blood spreading out from under their bodies, and it's only then that I understand.

They're dead.

But that isn't possible. The ARVN are our allies. We're fighting for them, to save their country from the communists in the North. Why would they shoot us?

One of them jams his muzzle into the small of my back and shoves me forward, past the MPs and over to a waiting truck.

I want to yell at him to stop, that he can't do that to me, that I'm an American! But I keep my mouth shut. The only smart thing I've done since coming to Vietnam. The soldier keeps jabbing at me, barking at me, gesturing at me to climb in the back of the truck. The sides are open. There are long benches on either side in the bed, with several Vietnamese men, a few of them in ARVN uniforms, already sitting there, their hands bound in front of them. I take a seat on one of the benches. No one looks at me. A couple of the soldiers climb into the cab. The rest climb into the back and keep their guns on me and the men who are bound.

The engine roars to life and the truck lurches forward. I nearly fall out of my seat.

My heart is racing. Sweat pours down my face. I want to tear the suit off and throw myself out of the truck and run away. But I can't move. The thoughts slowly, reluctantly, line up in my mind—thoughts I don't want to have but can't keep out any longer: If I don't do what they say—and maybe even if I do—they'll kill me, just like they killed the MPs. What I can't figure out, for the life of me, is why.

January 31, after midnight

The truck lurches through Cholon and all over Saigon, the driver grinding through the gears as if he's never driven stick before, doesn't know how to double-clutch, to keep up the RPMs, to keep from stalling out, which we also do over and over. Geoff's family has a car with a manual transmission, and he drove us out to the wilds of Long Island and showed me how to do all that stuff. I got whiplash then and I get it even worse now. Everyone in the back of the truck does.

There are other stops. Awful, horrible stops as we leave the congested streets of Cholon and slip into residential neighborhoods on avenues lined with towering hardwoods, thick stands of bamboo, and oceans of bougainvillea. One soldier is left to guard us while the rest storm up to a house or into a compound, their guns drawn. Sometimes there are sentries and shootouts. Sometimes there are walls that have to be scaled. Always there is the loud banging on doors, the crashing sound of doors kicked in. Shrill Vietnamese voices—protesting, pleading, screaming, begging. The pop-pop-pop of what I keep pretending are more fireworks, but I know aren't.

Sometimes there is more screaming. Sometimes there is just silence, which is even worse and makes my skin crawl. I start shaking as if it's cold out and can't make myself stop. Most of the bound men next to me are stoic, staring down between their shoes like those hunchbacked old men and women I saw earlier when I was in the tuk-tuk on my way to Bunny Bunny Go Go.

A few of the bound men are crying. Tears streaming down their faces like it's pouring rain. They don't make a sound from it, though. They just cry. About what's happening to the people in those houses and compounds. About what's going to happen soon to them, to all of us. I just want to be back where it's safe. The embassy. Our apartment in New York. We have a doorman, for God's sake. He won't let anyone in our building if we aren't there to vouch for them. Not a friend, not a service man, not the Viet Cong or the North Vietnamese Army.

The soldiers come back and the truck jerks forward again. But they keep stopping, again and again. Another house. Another compound. More crashing, banging, explosions, firecrackers, screaming, silence.

Only sometimes there aren't firecrackers. Sometimes the soldiers come back with more prisoners—some in street clothes, some in pajamas, some in uniforms. We squeeze closer to make room. And still nobody looks at anybody else. And as the night continues toward morning, it finally does turn cold, giving me a real reason to shiver.

In the distance, we hear bigger explosions, bigger fireworks lighting up the night sky all over the city. It's clear to me that we're with a team of assassins—executing government officials, military officers, prearranged targets. Even the ones who are taken prisoner—that must have been planned, too. But what about me? Why did they take me captive? I'm the only American. Is this all just a freak accident? Maybe they were looking for somebody else and just happened to stumble on me and the MPs. If they didn't know who I was before, they know now. They have my passport, my embassy papers, my name.

I keep hyperventilating and then telling myself to calm down, just calm down. I have to be steady. I have to keep my hopes up. Every minute that passes when they don't return and kill all the rest of us in the truck I take as evidence that they aren't going to kill us later, either. It must mean they have other plans for us. Hostages, maybe. Maybe they're just going to hold us for ransom, and then let us go. Maybe they know who Frank Sorenson is—the Special Attaché to Whatever—and they know Frank Sorenson will do whatever is necessary to get his son back.

But what if they attacked the embassy, too? Dad and Mom

could be in danger. Or captured like me. Or worse. I panic, can't stop trembling, bite my lip to keep from bawling out loud out of fear.

At one house, the last as it turns out, someone runs. Somehow he gets past the soldiers and sprints out into the street, after careening into the side of the truck. For just a second, our eyes meet—he looks shocked to see me, almost as if he recognizes me from somewhere, though that isn't possible—then he races off. It takes the guard a minute to react before he aims and fires, a loud burst of automatic gunfire spraying the asphalt behind the disappearing man. Somehow, miraculously, the man gets away. He's in his nightclothes, barefoot, but he keeps sprinting, maybe outrunning the bullets, or more likely just lucky, or saved by lousy aim.

From miles away, all over the city, I can hear battles raging. The assassins shrug, sling their weapons over their shoulders, and climb into the truck. We drive off into the night, but there are no more stops. I close my eyes and try praying, though Mom hasn't taken me to church in years, so the best I can come up with are bits and pieces of prayers I've heard other people say. I wish I hadn't been such a jerk to so many people, and I swear I'll be a better person if I get out of this. And if Mom and Dad survive as well. The man sitting next to me is whispering under his breath. I wonder if he's praying, too, and if it will make a difference.

We pull into what looks like a racetrack with a wide, grassy infield full of soldiers with automatic weapons, and dozens of mortars lined up behind concrete barriers, and a makeshift cage with hundreds of men and even some women crammed inside.

The truck stops next to the cage and guards order us out, shoving us hard from behind to force us in with the others. They hit us with bamboo staffs if we don't move fast enough. One blow lands on the back of my head, just behind my ear, and leaves me with a headache and a persistent ringing sound that I can't shake. I cling to the side of the cage and press my face against the wire so I can breathe, and so this claustrophobic feeling won't spiral out of control. My heart is pounding hard enough that I can hear it, even with the loud ringing in my ear, and I struggle to keep myself from bursting into tears and begging my captors to let me go.

Someone keeps pressing into my back, like he's leaning on a lamppost instead of another prisoner. I shove him away, but he slumps into me again. "Get off!" I snap, and shove him again. He doesn't say anything. Maybe he leans into somebody else for a while, but then he's back, and this time I can't push him off. I twist around so I can see him and say something directly to his face. His eyes are wide, staring straight at me, but no matter what I say he doesn't respond. I get angry and louder, but still nothing.

And then I realize there's blood. On him, on me, on my black suit, my tie, Dad's wing tip shoes. I feel all over myself to see if I've been wounded and haven't noticed, which is stupid, but I'm not thinking straight. I'm not thinking at all, until it hits me: *Oh God, he's dead.*

He's been shot, or bayoneted, or beaten so badly that all the life bled out of him. But he isn't dead enough, because he won't stop staring at me. I want him to close his eyes. More than I want to get away from him and all that blood, I want him to stop looking at me. If he's going to be dead, I want him to look dead, too. I can't explain why that's so important to me. Others around us back away, though it's inches, not feet. There isn't room. They speak to one another in whispered Vietnamese; I don't understand a word of it. I lift my hand tentatively to the dead man's face and press on his eyelids, afraid they'll be frozen open, but they aren't. They close as easily as if he blinked them shut himself. Other bodies shift in the cage, making a little more room, and the dead man slumps halfway to the ground. That's as far as his body can go, though, and he stays there, pushed against our legs as if he insisted on sitting down, just taking a rest.

I twist back around and press my face to the wire again as more trucks pull into the racetrack with more soldiers and more prisoners. The sky turns purple from the first light of morning. I just want to lie down and curl up in a ball. I've barely slept since leaving New York. I regret everything. Why did I sneak out? Why was I such a jerk to Mom and Dad? To that girl Cindy? I should have stayed. I should have thought about Beth and not messed around with Cindy in the first place. I shouldn't have been trying to impress Geoff. He isn't even here. I could have just made up some wild stories for him when I got back to New York. I could have stayed at the embassy. I could have been safe.

And now look where it's gotten me. There's blood on my hands, and I have nowhere to wipe it off.

January 31, morning

Small arms fire and then mortar fire erupt near the racetrack. We're still in Saigon, and I'm pretty sure we're still in Cholon. There have been explosions across the city throughout the night, but this is closer, though I can't see anything except the soldiers outside the cage setting up defensive positions behind the concrete barriers and trucks and some armored vehicles that also pulled in during the night.

"Light infantry," someone says in English, practically right in my ear. I turn to see another American, an adult, who has somehow worked his way through the crowd of prisoners, because I know he wasn't here before that.

"Whose?" I ask.

"American and South Viets," he says. "I'm guessing they're still several blocks away. Judging from the sounds. North Viets are returning fire. You can tell by the different sounds the automatic weapons make—our M16s and their AK-47s. I'm betting the North Viets are shooting from windows and rooftops of whatever high-rises are over there. Our mortars will take them out, but it'll be awhile."

I already know that about the M16s and the AK-47s. I know a lot about weapons, and a lot about the military, from when I was little and still hanging on to every word from my dad. You might say he and I bonded over the war. Though not over *this* war. Once this war started, my dad basically went MIA on Mom and me. It was like he was marking time, living with us for a handful of years in Paris, and for a few more back in New York, then he jumped at the chance to go off to another war. But I couldn't get enough of his World War II stories when I was a kid, as sanitized as they were so I wouldn't get freaked out by the horrors I read about later on my own. He'd been part of the invasion of Normandy on D-day. Fought in the Battle of the Bulge. Spoke German and worked in army intelligence. Interrogated Nazis after the fall of Berlin. Met my mom when she was a college student in postwar Paris and my grandfather, a big Eisenhower supporter, was ambassador to France.

Not that that's any help to me now.

"What's going to happen to us?" I ask this new American.

He shrugs. More explosions light up the early dawn sky, and he looks back over that way. He's wearing jeans and a T-shirt with blood splattered on it. He has a heavy five-o'clock shadow and more blood caked to the side of his face and in his thick black hair, which is way too long for the military or anybody who works at the embassy. But he's the only other American as far as I can see.

"How did they get you?" I ask.

"Wrong place, wrong time," he says. "Who are you, kid? How'd you end up in a mess like this?"

"Taylor Sorenson," I said.

He blinks at me. "Any relation to Frank Sorenson?" he asks. "He your dad by any chance?"

"Yeah," I say. "We got here three days ago. Me and my mom. For his birthday. Then there was a party at the embassy. I sort of cut out and didn't tell anybody."

"They got your passport, your ID?"

"Yeah," I say. "But there's so many people. They probably forgot who it belongs to by now. Right?"

There's a heavy barrage of small arms fire that starts and doesn't stop. We have to shout to hear each other.

"Don't tell them who you are if that's the case," he says. "You don't want them to put two and two together and figure out you're connected to Sorenson if they don't already know. Though I'd be surprised if they don't."

"Why?" I ask. "I don't understand. He just works at the embassy. What difference does it make? You think they'll, like, hold me for ransom?"

"Your dad does a lot more than just work at the embassy," he says. "So keep your mouth shut tight. They'll have to do something with us and hopefully that doesn't mean execute all of us right here in the middle of the infield like this. Not exactly the way to win hearts and minds. Hasn't worked for us, and won't work for them. Not like this. Not a public massacre."

"Execution?" I stutter. "Public massacre?" The words hit me like a fist in the gut.

He doesn't have an opportunity to respond—to reassure me that nothing like that could possibly happen, which is what I desperately want to hear—because the guards open the cage and wave some of us out and over to a section of the infield where dozens of stretchers hold wounded men, some just lying there, as still as death, some moaning and writhing in pain.

One of the guards barks orders in Vietnamese, which the stranger seems to understand because he grabs me by the shoulder and says, "Stick with me. We're loading these stretchers onto trucks."

Just as he says it, a couple of flatbeds pull up next to the wounded men. The stranger takes one end of the closest stretcher and I lift the other. At first I can't see what's wrong with the man we're carrying, but then the blanket falls and I see one of his legs has been blown off, his bloody, ragged stump leaking onto the stretcher. For some reason, the leg is lying on the stretcher, too, next to him. The boot is still on the foot. I'm so shocked I nearly drop my end. The leg is raw and bloody and mutilated, with shattered bone protruding out of the flesh. Bile rises up my throat and into my mouth, making me gag.

"Come on!" the stranger barks. "Don't draw attention to yourself!"

I force myself to swallow it back down. We hand the wounded man up to other prisoners in the back of the first truck—military green, US Army insignia on the side.

"Stolen," the stranger says.

"But why would the South Vietnamese steal from us?" I ask. "Why are they attacking us? And their own people? We're on the same side. Is it a coup?"

"No," he says. "These aren't South Viets. They're regular army North Viets. Some of them dressed up in South Viet Army uniforms they also must have stolen. They attacked all over Saigon. They even attacked the embassy. Broke through the wall. Killed a bunch of marines. I don't know what's been happening there since."

"But my mom and dad are there," I say. "Do you think the attackers got inside? Do you think my mom and dad got out first?"

"Sorry, kid," he says as we lift the next stretcher. The man lying on it is already dead. He has a massive chest wound that's disgusting, shards of bone and slices of organs spilling out through the rags of his uniform. They didn't bother to cover him with a blanket. But we load him on the flatbed anyway. I keep my eyes averted and try not to throw up.

"You mean they did get in the embassy?" I manage to ask, not wanting to hear the answer if it's bad.

"Just mean I wasn't there to see what else happened," he says.

The street fighting grows louder and closer. Soon mortar rounds are coming over the racetrack wall and exploding in the turf, leaving craters and bodies. Men crawl in retreat to the concrete barriers, dragging their friends with them. With the light of morning and dissipating fog, I can see body parts strewn everywhere.

We keep loading the trucks with the wounded and the dead and the dying as the sun rises and it gets hotter. I'm parched, but there's no water—at least not for us. I can feel my face starting to blister under the burning sun, and despite how freaked out I am, my stomach rumbles. But there's no food, either. If I stop working, a guard hits me with his bamboo staff—across my shoulders, on my arms or legs, anywhere that's exposed. I cover my face and head and keep working. The stranger never stops, doesn't react when they hit me, doesn't say anything else.

We're ordered onto one of the trucks with the wounded men and the bodies—and armed guards. A convoy of trucks pulls out of the racetrack, away from the gun and mortar battle, and we lumber through narrow Cholon streets, picking up speed gradually until soon we're careening around corners in tight intersections, smashing roadside stands. People peek at us from upper-story windows or half-open doors at street level, but few are out on the streets. Chickens fly into windshields and feathers spray all over. Dogs limp out of the way if they're fast enough and get crushed to the road if they aren't. The trucks never slow down, not even when we finally leave the sprawl of Saigon and bounce down washboard roads through the countryside, heading east into the late morning sun.

"Just keep your head down," the stranger says at one point. "Don't look at the guards. Don't do or say anything besides whatever they want you to do, even if you're not sure what that is. They don't speak English, in case you haven't figured that out yet."

"But you speak some Vietnamese," I say. "Right?"

He nods. "Some. Enough to get by."

I ask him his name. "I mean, what should I call you?"

"Let's go with TJ," he says.

"Just initials?" I ask.

"Yeah," he says. "Just initials. Better that they don't know who I am, and better you don't, either, so they can't get it out of you. Let's just say I've been doing work over here they don't like and I don't want them knowing about it."

"Okay," I say. "TJ." Then I ask him, "Do you really think they'll kill us?"

He studies the blur of landscape as we sweep past, trees so close that branches slap the sides of the truck—and us, if we don't duck in time.

"I shouldn't have said that," he finally answers. "But it's a possibility. The longer they don't, the more likely they won't, is the way I see it. Unless something changes, some part of the equation."

"Like what?" I ask.

"Like they find out who I am, or who you are—or who your dad is. But then again, that might work in your favor. They might think you're worth something to them."

"Worth something?"

"Prisoner exchange," he says. "That sort of thing. But they'd need to stash you someplace, and I don't know where that would be. Maybe in the North."

"In North Vietnam?" I say in a panic. "But how?"

The truck bounces through a deep rut in the road. Some of the wounded NVA soldiers are thrown off their stretchers and the guards motion for us to help them back up.

After we get them settled again and discover another one who has died during the journey, TJ explains. "West is Cambodia. Northwest is Laos. North is North Vietnam. Simple geography.

The North Viets have a secret trail that crosses the border and goes up through Cambodia and Laos. It's how they got all their soldiers down here to attack Saigon and how they've been supplying the guerrilla army, the Viet Cong, all these years down here in the South. It's been their supply line throughout the war."

"If it's a secret trail, then how come you know about it?" I ask.

He laughs. "It's a secret trail that everybody knows about," he says. "Except that they sort of do and they sort of don't. The US can't legally cross the border to do anything about it. And anyway, it's not just one trail, it's a whole network of trails, and the ones they use change all the time, and most of them are camouflaged, and some are so deep inside Cambodia and Laos that even if we—or the South Viets—do cross the border to go after them, it isn't possible to go that far, because it would be considered an invasion, and there's no government authorization for that. Even air raids have limited success. And believe me, we've flown hundreds of them. Thousands."

We're deep into the countryside now, with wide swaths of green rice paddies spreading out from the sides of the narrow road. "The North Viets call it the Reunification Trail," TJ says. "They also call it Blood Road. Because they've shed so much blood on it—building it, defending it, transporting troops and supplies down it. They even strap bags of gas and oil to their people and have them carry it down the Trail since there's no pipeline. Not yet, anyway. Our side calls it the Ho Chi Minh Trail. You probably got that from the newspapers back in the States? Or on the nightly news?"

I shake my head. "I guess I haven't been paying too much attention."

TJ spits off the side of the truck as we slow down in the middle of nowhere. "You do know who Ho Chi Minh is, don't you?" he asks.

"Yeah, sure," I say. "President of North Vietnam. Everybody knows that."

"Close enough," TJ says. "Anyway, looks like we're here."

We stop under a small copse of trees on an island at the center of more acres of green rice paddies spreading out on both sides of the narrow dirt road. I'm guessing we're maybe twenty miles outside Saigon. A boy sits on the back of a water buffalo in the middle of one of the rice paddies, his face shadowed by his wide conical hat. In the distance, maybe half a mile away, is a green wall of thick jungle. Red dust envelops us from the dry road and breathing it leaves me parched—too dry to form any saliva and spit it out. My tongue feels swollen.

TJ points to the green wall. "I'm guessing that's where we're going."

January 31, afternoon

Guards swing their bamboo staffs to herd us out of the truck—me, TJ, and a dozen other prisoners, all Vietnamese. I should have figured out already why we're here, but I don't put two and two together until they order us to lift the stretchers and carry them single file along narrow dikes through the rice paddies toward the distant hills. TJ says the North Viets must have a hospital hidden over there to treat their casualties from the fighting in Saigon. I nod and keep my head down. Any time we slow, guards sprint up next to us, knee deep in the water, their AK-47s slung over their shoulders, and strike harder with their bamboo staffs. I have blisters on my feet from Dad's dress shoes. I want to peel off the suit coat I still have on, but I'm afraid to stop and put down my end of the stretcher, so I continue, sweating profusely until I'm too dehydrated to even do that. The dirty, stagnant water in the rice paddies starts to look good, but there's no way to stop, and I take my cue from TJ, who marches ahead at a pace that seems to please the guards but is killing me.

The man on our stretcher suddenly moans and opens his eyes. He winces in pain with every step we take and presses his hand to his heavily bandaged side. Blood has seeped through the bandages, and he lifts his hand to his face and seems surprised to see it covered in red. TJ's face, which was crusted in blood when I first saw him, is openly bleeding now, too. When it gets in his eyes, he stops and wipes his face on his T-shirt. I pull off my paisley tie and knot it into a headband.

The sun is a merciless ball directly overhead, burning what's left of my brain.

Eventually the rice paddies end and we enter the jungle—so thick I can't see a way through. Once we're there, though, an opening, just wide enough for us to pass inside, materializes and to anyone watching from the trucks back on the red dirt road it probably looks like we just suddenly disappear. It's darker in here, with overhanging trees, impossible to see more than a few feet into the foliage. The path twists and turns, runs straight for a while, then seems to run the other way, the way we just came. Another trail branches off, then another.

A soldier stands guard where the path makes yet another sudden turn. He wears a wide-brimmed conical hat like the peasants in the fields. He points and we follow the stretcher-bearers in front still deeper into the jungle. The path dips slightly, to a trickle of water that was probably a true stream before this winter drought—and no doubt will be again when it's the rainy season. TJ says something in Vietnamese to the guard. The guard looks around before nodding.

"It's okay to get a drink," TJ says. I hesitate at first, because as desperately thirsty as I am, all I heard from Mom for the past three days was how I wasn't to drink the water, no matter what, unless it was boiled for twenty minutes first.

TJ lies flat on his belly and scoops handfuls up to his parched lips, and I decide better to catch some disease than die of thirst. The guard brings a canteen to the wounded man and holds it to his mouth, though most of it dribbles down his cheeks.

The guard pokes us with his bamboo staff. We stand up from the water reluctantly. He waves at us with his AK-47, so we pick up the stretcher again. I brace myself for miles of the same, but a few minutes later we're standing at an opening in the ground I might have walked right over if another North Viet guard hadn't been standing there, gesturing for us to lower the wounded man inside.

Peering into the hole, I see several of the men from the truck, our fellow prisoners. TJ and I hand our stretcher down, then climb in after it to an enormous underground room, with wood and rope beds, kerosene lamps, and crude operating tables, every one of them holding a bleeding man or woman, surrounded by a team of doctors or nurses or whatever they are—none wear surgical masks or scrubs or gowns or anything that makes them look medical, just NVA uniforms or what look like black pajama pants and shirts like I saw earlier on people working in the rice paddies.

We pick up our stretcher again and carry it to a triage area, and as my eyes adjust to the semi-dark I see armed soldiers everywhere, food cooking in large iron pots over small fires, cisterns full of water, tables and chairs, and more lanterns, and entrances to other rooms or tunnels shooting off from the hospital area. Somebody shoves small plates of rice and grub worms at TJ and me and the Vietnamese prisoners who've brought in other stretchers. I hesitate, but the others dig in, scooping the food with their fingers. Two minutes later, a guard snatches the plates, and I have time to shove a fistful of rice in my mouth before the guard gets mine, too. He finishes what's left as he walks away with the tin plates.

Then they're back at us with their bamboo staffs, shooing us out of the underground and into the harsh sunlight.

"What now?" I ask TJ.

"More stretchers," he says. "That's my guess."

I want him to keep talking to me, but he lapses into silence after that and we plod back down the trail. I wish I could shut off my brain, but every few minutes, my anxiety spikes so high I find it hard to get a good breath. I'm afraid that at any second one of the guards will turn his weapon on me. I'm afraid they might have already killed Mom and Dad. I'm afraid they're going to take me to North Vietnam and nobody will ever know what happened to me. I'm afraid I'll never see my family again, or my friends, or anybody. Never go home to New York, or hear any more bands, or swim on the swim team, or hang out with Geoff, or learn how to drive a car.

I'm afraid I'll never get to live my actual life. I keep picturing the guy whose leg got shot off, the dead man with the chest wound, the poor military police back in Saigon who ended up dead in the street, all because of me.

The trucks are gone when we return to the road, but there are dozens of stretchers still there, hidden in that copse of trees. We pick up a man whose head and face are so heavily bandaged that I can barely make out the contours of his mouth and nose. Half his clothes have been burned off, and one of his arms and one of his legs and part of his torso are black and charred and oozing pus. The rancid smell from the wounds is even worse than looking at them, and I gag.

"Get it together," TJ hisses at me. "Don't make a scene."

I swallow hard, then lift my end. I ache all over and just want to drop my side and lie down. But off we go, over the dikes and through the rice paddies and the long, searing half mile back to the green wall of jungle and the underground hospital. I'm too tired to say anything to TJ until we climb back out, and once again get to stop at the little stream. "If they bring us to North Vietnam, how far is that?" I ask TJ. "How long would it take?"

"Weeks. Maybe months," he says, glancing over to keep an eye on the guards watching us. "They wouldn't waste using their transport vehicles to get us there, so we'd be walking the Trail the whole way. Under armed guard. My guess is it would just be you and me, and any other Americans they've captured."

"What about these other guys?" I ask. "These South Vietnamese prisoners?"

"They'll keep them around as long as they're useful," he says.

"What about when they're not useful anymore?"

"Like I said, they'll keep them around as long as they're useful, but they won't let them go. Maybe some prisoners will try to defect, to save themselves. Try to convince the North Viets that they want to join the cause. But that probably won't happen."

"And what happens to us once we're in the North? Where would they take us exactly?" I ask.

"Probably the Hanoi Hilton," he says.

I can't tell if he's being serious. "Is it nice?"

He laughs a dry laugh. "It's not what you think," he says. "They only call it that. It's a prison. Where they keep American prisoners of war. Pilots they shot down. Long-range reconnaissance guys that got captured. You see those POWs making

56

propaganda statements on the news, about how America shouldn't be in the war and they're sorry they took part in bombing Hanoi and the poor, innocent North Vietnamese people? Those guys are in the Hanoi Hilton. Not a fun place."

I know what he's talking about. I've seen some of those captured American pilots on the news, wearing striped pajamas with their hair chopped off. They were dirty and weary and thin as skeletons, with dark, cavernous circles around their eyes. They read statements denouncing the American war effort, but not like they meant it.

We finish our trip back into the jungle and the twisting path, once again lowering the stretcher carefully into the dark hole, then climbing down and carrying the wounded man into the triage area. It's hard negotiating the rough ground coming from blinding light to half night, and even harder stumbling out back into the glare of the afternoon. But we aren't allowed to stop.

"Look, there might be a way out of this," TJ whispers to me as we stumble back onto the path. "Up ahead here, there's maybe a fifty-meter stretch where they don't have any guards posted, a big curve in the trail, and there's no visibility from ahead or behind. When I give the signal, we dive off the trail. It's going to be a steep plunge down the side, and it's going to hurt. There's a chance we can get some distance between us and them before they realize we've escaped."

"And then what?" I ask. "What do we do after that?"

"Then we run," he says.

I'm not at all sure about this plan, if you can even call it that, and I have a hundred questions about how it can possibly work. It sounds insane. Desperate and insane. But before I can say anything else, we're there.

"Ready?" TJ asks. We're in the clear, at least for the moment.

He doesn't wait for me to say, just plunges off the trail the way he said he would, and goes crashing through the brush.

I freeze. I should follow him, but I just can't. I don't know why. It's too sudden. I'm too scared. Too much of a coward.

The guards are suddenly next to me, yelling and pointing. One hits me hard behind my knees with his bamboo staff and I crumple to the ground. He keeps beating me, and I curl up in a ball and cover my head until he stops. After, I just lie there whimpering, my clothes torn, dust in my eyes, blood in my mouth.

There's more yelling as they chase TJ. A three-round burst of automatic weapon fire. Then more shouting. Then nothing.

I can't believe it. Just minutes before, TJ was the one person I could sort of depend on to help me survive all this. And now he's dead. And now I have nobody.

January 31, evening

The guards pair me up with a Vietnamese prisoner who looks as frightened as I feel, and we spend the remaining daylight hours trudging back and forth between the road and the underground hospital. More trucks come with more casualties from Saigon. Part of me feels terrible for all the wounded men and women. Part of me wants them all to die for what they did to the MPs, and to TJ, and to the marines at the embassy, and to who knows how many others.

People speak to one another in Vietnamese—guards yelling orders, prisoners whispering. I stay silent, desperately alone, with no one to talk to and no idea what's going on without TJ.

At one point late in the day they grab me and my new partner and march us into the jungle to bury TJ. I don't know why they just left him there all that time. They don't bother to explain, and I couldn't understand them anyway. I try not to look at TJ's body, or to step in the pool of blood that seeps into the dry earth. There aren't any shovels, just sticks they hand us, and then point to where we're supposed to dig. It will be a shallow grave at best, and I'm sure whatever animals live in these woods will be able to get at the body without any trouble. But I'm still glad when they tell us to stop. I've been working hard to shut down my brain, to ward off a full-blown panic attack. It helps that I'm so exhausted, so woozy from the hunger and dehydration, that I can barely stand up. I grab TJ under his arms and lift. His head rolls back in this ghastly way. His whole body, everything about him, is limp and dead heavy. My Vietnamese partner takes TJ's feet. Even together we aren't strong enough to lift him all the way off the ground, so we half carry, half drag him to the hole and roll him in. I stack as many stones as I can over him, covering his face first so I won't have to look at it anymore, then we push dirt back on top of the stones and then we're done.

═══════════════════════════

There is no more rice or grubs on tin plates when we finish our work that night. The guards march us deep into the jungle, away from the underground hospital, where they tie us to a tree, me and a half dozen other prisoners, our backs pressed into the rough bark, our shoulders jabbing into one another. Our unhappy guards sit nearby, their guns on their knees as they smoke cigarettes and talk in the growing dark. They give us a single canteen of dirty water. I'm the last to get it, and by the time it makes its way around the circle of prisoners, each of them taking a drink and then handing it off to whoever is next, it's empty except for a few drops I manage to shake out on my tongue. The man next to me, the one who finished off the last of the water, won't look at me. It doesn't matter. There's nothing I can do, but that doesn't stop me from complaining to the guard. "He drank it all!" I shake the empty canteen at him, desperate for him to understand and offer more water.

He ignores me.

Our hands are tied in front of us, with a longer rope threaded behind our elbows, binding us all together and to the tree. I don't think it will be possible to sleep. I'm too hungry and thirsty and traumatized by everything I saw the night before and through- out this awful day. Too haunted by the images of the dead mili- tary police and TJ. I was in a fight once, in seventh-grade gym class. It was during a basketball game. Somebody fouled me, and one thing led to another and somebody said something and I said something back, and the next thing I knew we were rolling on the gym floor, punching at each other. I got a fat lip. The other kid's nose got broken, and the coach came over and got him to stop crying long enough to use his thumbs to straighten out the cartilage.

I had nightmares about seeing that kid's face for weeks after and didn't want to go back to school. I thought I was a terrible person for what I'd done to him, even though he was pretty much fine and over it in a couple of days.

And that was it—my entire history of violence, except for stuff I'd seen in the movies and on TV and on the news. But that stuff didn't count. That stuff was all pretend, or far enough away that it amounted to the same thing.

This, though—this is different. I have dried blood on me from the man who died in the cage back at the racetrack. My clothes are also covered in TJ's blood. And I still have it on my hands. And I have welts all over from the beatings by the guards with their bamboo staffs.

Yet even with all of that, I sleep. They might still be planning to kill me tomorrow, or start the long march with me to Hanoi, but one last thought I have as I slip under is that at least I survived today.

I wake up in total darkness, disoriented, thrashing, confused that I can't move my hands or my body, just my legs, flailing wildly until someone kicks me back hard in the shin to get me to stop. I freeze, remembering where I am, slowly coming out of the fog of deep sleep as night sounds crescendo around me. Insects, night birds, crawling things in the brush, wind in the trees. My eyes adjust slowly. I rub them with my bound hands and try to blink out the dust. I can't swallow. My mouth and throat are too dry. I have to pee, only there's no way to do it. I can't get up, can't walk away from the tree and the other prisoners, can't ask the guards to let me loose so I can go—even if I knew where they were.

I hold it for as long as I can, but then give up and pee on myself. It's warm at first but quickly turns cold. I try to pull what's left of my suit coat tighter around me, thankful in the chill of deep night or predawn morning that I didn't toss it away the day before, even though I sweated through it over and over. I spend the next hour, or however long it is, hating the man beside me, the one who finished off the water in the canteen. All I can think about is how thirsty I am, so desperate to drink that I would do anything, give up anything, for just a sip of water.

Finally, mercifully, the guards come back with another canteen and this time I'm first. I want to drink it all, every last drop, but the man on my other side is already grasping for the water with his bound hands. He can't reach all the way because of how we're tied up. I can keep it all for myself and make up for the miserable night and pay them all back for cheating me the day before.

But then a guard snatches the canteen out of my hands and shoves it at my neighbor. He stands watching as the prisoners each have their drink and pass it on. And then, once the canteen makes it all the way around the tree, he unties us. It doesn't make any sense. Why not let us loose before? It isn't like anybody is going to run off. My legs are cramping so bad that I can barely stand, and my shoulders are so stiff I can't lift my arms. All of us stagger around the small clearing, trying to get the blood circulating.

Another guard comes with a pot of sticky rice. The other prisoners hold out their hands. Each gets two fistfuls, which they stuff in their mouths right away, maybe worried that somebody will steal it if they don't. I take a small bite of mine and chew for as long as I can, and then another, and another, until, sadly, it's gone. My stomach rumbles, and I have to go to the bathroom. I pantomime for the guard, to get his permission. I know enough by now not to try to do anything without their okay. He laughs and points to a bush, and then stands over me while I squat and do my business. I ignore him, past caring about things like privacy that no longer exist.

Afterward, they march us down a narrow path back to the hospital. The stench hits well before we get there—of rotting flesh and buckets of blood—and I'm not the only one who gags as the guards herd us inside. There are as many stretchers full of wounded men, women, and teenagers as there were the day before. We have a different job this morning, though: collecting piles of amputated limbs and carrying them outside to burn or bury. I freeze for a second and then bend over, dry heaving until a guard strikes me with his bamboo staff across my shoulders and knocks me to the stone floor. They jerk me back to my feet. Sticky rice comes up in my throat and I'm afraid I'll lose it, so I force myself to swallow it back down, though it leaves a bitter acid taste in my mouth.

We place as many of the severed limbs as will fit on torn sections of tarpaulin and carry them aboveground, then down another hidden path deep into the jungle, where we drop them in a large hole. A guard throws lime powder over each load of arms and legs and feet and hands, covering every new layer as we add them to the pit. I think about the poet Walt Whitman's description of a similar pile of severed body parts—"human fragments, cut, bloody, black and blue, swelled and sickening"—under a gnarled catalpa tree outside a mansion-turned-combat-hospital in Virginia during the Civil War. We read it in literature class last year, a lifetime ago.

And here it is a hundred years later, another war halfway around the world, and it looks like nothing has changed.

February 1

I spend most of the day panicking about Mom and Dad and the attack on the embassy. I tie my coat around my waist and refasten my tie around my head, and for hours without stopping we carry more stretchers from the road through the rice paddies to the jungle, or we carry more pieces of men and women that no longer matter out to the lime pit. All of it reminds me that the battle must still be raging back in Saigon, but not knowing anything about it—and especially about what happened at the embassy—is making me crazy. Mom and I haven't gotten along in forever, and neither have me and Dad, since he abandoned me for the war in Vietnam, but they're still my parents.

They let us drink out of the filthy stream that TJ and I drank from the day before, but there's no more food, no sticky rice, no nothing. The guards no longer follow us so closely, and they don't hit us with their bamboo staffs. I guess they figure they have us trained well enough by now that none of it is necessary. And since they killed TJ, everybody knows what will happen if they try to escape.

It's funny how even the most awful things—carrying amputated limbs, corpses, and dying people, with their horrible wounds and gross smells and awful noises—can become not normal, exactly, but not abnormal. You don't get used to it, but you don't freak out about it, either. Not after a while. Not after a couple of days. Maybe exhaustion makes you deaf and blind, or maybe your senses just turn off because you can't take anything else in. All I know is that I'm numb, but I keep walking, keep carrying stretchers, keep drinking from that stream, keep filling the tarp with body parts, keep putting one foot in front of the other. My brain even shuts down, so that I eventually quit worrying about Mom and Dad, or anybody or anything. I just want to finish the trek I'm on and get back to that stream, back to that water, and drink and rest, and nothing else matters.

Except that, from time to time, the panic hits me again, never far from the surface. And then, in those flashes, it's all I can do to keep from collapsing in a little heap and crying for my mom and begging the guards to let me go see her and make sure she's all right—or yell at the guards that my dad is going to come looking for me and they better be ready when he finds me, because he's going to make them pay in all kinds of terrible ways for what they've done.

Several of the prisoners do collapse when we're out in the broiling sun, negotiating the dikes through the rice paddies. They stumble, sag to their knees, carefully place or drop their end of the stretcher, and then fall forward or pitch sideways into the dank water and the rice shoots. Sometimes the guards pull them up and they regain their balance. Sometimes the guards have to drag them to some small spot of shade to let them rest. One man falls and doesn't get back up. They drag him away. We never see him again.

Late in the afternoon, in the bunker where we've just brought another wounded NVA soldier, they let us sit, and then seem to forget we're there, shuffled to the side, our backs against the wall. A couple of the prisoners fall asleep, slumped over on their sides on the stone floor. I just sit there, slack-jawed, dully watching the frenzied activity as the doctors run from patient to patient and fight to remove shell fragments and bullets and shattered bones and shredded tissue and all those arms and legs and feet we'll be carrying off soon enough to the lime pit.

I'm vaguely aware of people climbing down into the hospital, an NVA patrol pausing at the bottom of the ladder, surveying what's going on, and then making their way deeper inside—and over to our little squad of prisoners. They stop in front of us. I try not to look up—TJ warned me not to make eye contact—but there's something deeply familiar about one of the new soldiers. And the way he's gazing, hard, makes me think he sees something familiar in me as well. And then it hits me, shaking me from my stupor.

"Hanh!" I shout, jumping to my feet. It's Dad's driver!

"What are you doing here?" I say, my voice way too loud. I'm so excited to see him, sure that he's here for me. "Did you come to get me?"

Hanh frowns, takes another step forward, and slaps me so hard that I fall back to the floor, sprawling into the other prisoners.

I just lie there for a minute, not moving, not seeing or hearing anything, my mind blank. When the fog lifts, I pull myself into a seated position and press my hand to my burning cheek. Hanh glares at me, then turns away to confer with some other soldiers. After a few minutes, he turns around to look at me again. A young woman wearing the loose black clothing instead of a uniform—but still carrying an AK-47—turns with him. I crab-walk back, afraid he's going to hit me again.

"Stop cowering," Hanh says. "Get up. No one will hurt you—as long as you do what you're told."

I struggle to my feet but keep as much distance between us as I can. Most of the activity has stopped.

"What are you going to do to me?" I ask in a shaky voice. "And can you tell me, about my mother—"

"I know nothing about her," he says.

"But is she alive? And my dad?" I ask. "Can you just tell me that? Please?"

"I know nothing about them," he says again, his voice even, his face impassive. "Do not ask again." He nods at the girl. "You will go with this soldier, Comrade Phuong Tram. That is all you need to know."

He looks me up and down, then says something in Vietnamese to Phuong. He turns back to me. "In America you can be a stupid, foolish boy and nothing will come of it. You think you can do whatever you like. You think the world belongs to you. Do not make the mistake of thinking you can be so stupid and foolish here."

He turns on his heel and leaves. Phuong and two young Vietnamese soldiers, wearing all black like her, stay. One of them hands her a length of bamboo with a rope threaded through it and a noose on the end. I back farther away, stones in the wall cutting into my back, convinced they're going to hang me. I beg them to please, please don't, but I'm helpless to stop them. The two young soldiers grab my arms and hold me while Phuong fits the noose over my head and tightens it around my throat—tight enough that I can feel it, but not so tight that I can't breathe or swallow or speak. The other soldier ties my hands behind my back. I'm trembling so hard that I can't stand on my own. The rope cuts into my neck when my knees start to buckle.

But it's not what I think. Phuong steps behind me, the end of the bamboo prodding me in the back of my neck, and she forces me forward. Too fast and the rope chokes me. Too slow and I get stabbed by the bamboo. We head east on a narrow trail into the jungle.

I remember what TJ told me about the Ho Chi Minh Trail and the Hanoi Hilton, and my heart sinks. I trip and fall forward. The noose jerks my head back and bites into my throat, cutting off my air. I flop helplessly on the ground, trying to breathe and not panic, until the two soldiers grab me under my arms and pull me to my feet. Phuong gives me a minute, then forces me on down the trail, with stones and roots and vines everywhere to trip me again and again. I pitch forward a second time and nearly land on my face, but somehow manage to catch myself, though I stagger sideways into a thornbush. The thorns rip away what's left of one sleeve of my coat and rake my arm bloody. Phuong loosens the noose a little. I hope I'll see something like sympathy in her eyes, but instead it looks more like hate.

February 1, late afternoon

We're an hour from the underground hospital when we hear, screaming through the air, the earsplitting sound of jets. Explosions rip the world somewhere behind us. Fireballs erupt into the sky. Plumes of white smoke. The jets roar past, low to the ground, then circle back toward the hospital, or the rice paddies, or the road to Saigon: too far away to know. There are more explosions, more fireballs, more smoke. The ground shakes like an earthquake. We all fall.

Phuong is the first to stand, staring hard as if she can see beyond the trees and the brush. The other two guards pull themselves up as well. They tug at her sleeve to get her to go, but she won't move. They yank me to my feet, both their faces twisted with worry. The jets circle overhead one more time and then turn back toward Saigon. The white smoke turns black, and the sky grows dark as the haze kills the afternoon sun.

We walk for hours afterward. The sky eventually clears, leaving us exposed under the blazing sun, or gasping for air under the stifling shade of overhanging trees that form a winding tunnel through forest, the bushes and bamboo stands and grasses on either side of the trail so thick it makes me claustrophobic.

I beg them—beg Phuong—to untie my hands and take off the noose, but she ignores me. They all do. My neck is rubbed raw from the rope, and with every step the chafing worsens. I can't see, but imagine rivulets of blood streaming from my throat down the front of my shirt. I can't feel my hands. I pee myself again as we continue the march. Phuong and the others never seem to tire. They never stop. They never drink from their canteens. Not for those first hours after the bombings. They wear the straw hats so the sun doesn't bake their heads the way it does mine. I still have the paisley tie around my forehead, partly shading my eyes, but nothing for my sunburned nose and dried, cracked lips.

I try yet again: "Please let me go. I promise I won't try to escape."

Then I remember some Vietnamese people speak French, since France ran their country for, like, sixty years. Maybe Phuong does, too. Or one of the other soldiers. Mom made sure I learned French practically from the minute I was born when we lived in Paris.

So I ask Phuong again: "S'il vous plaît, laissez-moi partir. Je promets que je n'essaierai pas de m'échapper." *Please let me go. I promise I won't try to escape.*

She stops. The others stop. I stop. And the next thing I know, my hands are untied and the noose is off.

"Je vous remercie," I say, rubbing the feeling back into my wrists. I don't want to touch the raw skin around my throat. *Thank you.*

Phuong hands me her canteen, and I drink as much as I think I can get away with. The others drink from their canteens, too.

She shrugs and says, "Si vous courez, nous vous tirerons dessus." *If you run, we will shoot you.*

═══════════════════

We keep going until dusk. The hours in between we spend skirting the edges of more rice paddies, ducking into leafy tunnels that wind through more jungle so thick I can't see any of the animals I think I hear snuffling off in the brush. We finally stop to rest, and I lean against the trunk of a tall tree with low branches. A snake slides off one of the branches and onto my shoulder. I freeze. It's small and green and has what look like white lips. Phuong sees it and she freezes, too. The others don't notice. They're busy rolling and then sharing a cigarette.

The snake sits on my shoulder for what feels like an hour, but is probably not even a full minute, then winds its way down my torso and my leg and onto the ground. It slithers into the brush. I don't breathe from the second I feel it until well after it's gone.

A faint smile of relief crosses Phuong's face, just for an instant, and then she goes back to the stoic mask she's been wearing.

In French I ask her what kind of snake it was. She answers in Vietnamese, then, switching languages, saying she doesn't know the right name for it in French. "Vipère, peut-être."

I understand *viper* all right.

"Is it poisonous?" I ask.

"Un peu," she says. *A little.*

━━━━━━━━━━━━━━━━

I think we'll stop here for the night, much as I don't want to after just having a viper crawl all over me. But Phuong insists that we push on farther, which is crazy. It grows darker and darker, especially as we descend under another thick canopy of overhanging trees. With no flashlight or torch or even a match to light the path, Phuong seems to be feeling her way forward. Our progress slows to a crawl. I'm bone weary and don't mind the shuffling pace, though all I want to do is sleep.

When we finally stop, we all collapse on the ground. Phuong lets me drink again from her canteen. From somewhere in his pack, one of the soldiers produces cold sticky rice and peppers, which he shares with Phuong and the other soldier. Phuong places half of hers in my hands, though the soldiers give her disapproving looks. I eat as slowly as I can once again, trying to make it last as long as possible to trick my stomach or my brain into thinking it's a bigger meal. I sit beside a tree but keep a safe snake-distance from the trunk. We're in the middle of a small copse a few meters from the trail. Phuong positions one of the men in a sentry position a short way from us, closer to the path, then comes back over and settles on the ground to eat. All they carry are their weapons, ammunition belts, canteens, trenching tools, small packs slung over their shoulders, and what appear to be US Army–issued ponchos.

Phuong and the other soldier wrap themselves in their ponchos, tuck their AK-47s and gear in with them, and fall asleep. I lie on my side and curl up the way I've been wanting to all afternoon, but sleep eludes me. As tired as I am, the sights and sounds and smells of the past two days come crashing back down. I go spinning off into a terrified place where I can't stop thinking about all the blood on me. What if there are more snakes here, more vipers, and they can smell it?

After what must be hours, there's a soft rustling as the soldier next to Phuong rouses himself and gathers his poncho and equipment and goes off for his turn keeping watch. Phuong mutters something in her sleep. The other soldier comes back. Finally, distracted from my paranoia about the snakes and the blood, I melt to the hard ground, pull the remnants of my suit coat over my head, and sleep.

February 2

We stop at midmorning the next day. Phuong seems to be puzzling over our location. She leaves the trail for a while, maybe half an hour, leaving me with the other soldiers. I've figured out their names: Trang, the tall, dour one, and Vu, who is several inches shorter and wears a perpetual grin, as if anticipating somebody saying something funny just so he can laugh, though I haven't heard him laugh even once so far.

Not that there's been anything to laugh about. The jets. The bombs. Their friends in the underground hospital, or driving transport vehicles . . .

Phuong emerges quietly from the brush and motions for us to follow, so we plunge in behind her, Trang, then me, then Vu, who is practically riding on my back and keeps stepping on my heels, which are blistered and sore and hurt even when I'm not walking. I finally stop suddenly and he rams into my back. I snarl at him, which is a stupid thing to do to a guy holding a fully loaded AK-47. He takes a step back and mutters what I take to be an apology. He keeps his grin the whole time.

Phuong pauses in a small clearing not long after that. She looks around in a way somebody might if they're about to share a big secret; Vu and Trang do the same. They confer with one another, and then Phuong bends over and lifts a small door, a hatch, that's just lying there flat on the jungle floor, right in front of us, covered with dirt and leaves. I could have walked over it a hundred times and not noticed it was there, just like before. Only something tells me it's not going to be a hospital we'll be climbing down into.

Then, as if on cue, several heavily camouflaged NVA soldiers materialize out of the forest, weapons drawn. Phuong speaks to one of them, who nods. The camouflaged soldiers then retreat into the brush.

"Follow me," Phuong says in French as she eases herself down, feeling her way to the invisible rungs of a ladder. Vu steps aside and points for me to go next, but the last thing in the world I want to do is follow Phuong into that hole. I think of the French word—*oubliette*—which means dungeon, only a special kind of dungeon where you're thrown in from an opening in the ceiling, or from a hanging staircase that goes partway down but stops. One way in, no way out.

Vu cuffs me on the side of my head. Trang jabs me in the small of my back with his gun. I go down.

The rickety ladder is just rough wood—sticks, really—lashed together with hemp and feels as if it might fall apart at any second. The hole grows lighter near the bottom as we descend, though there is no visible light source. An NVA soldier stands guard at the bottom, his weapon pointed straight at my face when I finally reach the ground. Phuong plunges off into a narrow tunnel and I follow. My shoulders scrape the walls and if I don't lean forward, my head hits the ceiling.

There are dim lanterns. More guards. More branches off the tunnel. Rooms over to the side with soldiers studying maps on a small table, others quietly eating their meager rations of sticky rice, men squatting in a circle, doing nothing, women, maybe nurses, tending to the wounded lying on thin pallets on the stone floor, their eyes pressed shut, their faces glistening with sweat—Phuong says from malaria or infection—though it's cold so far underground. Cold and close.

As my eyes adjust and we trek deeper into the bowels of the tunnel complex, I see ventilation tubes protruding from the walls and ceiling, small cookstoves in corners, an operating room with bloody sheets littering the floor. A body. Another body.

Phuong pulls me into one of the side tunnels, down another long wood-and-hemp ladder, through a dank section where brown water leeches from the walls and puddles on the floor, running off in tiny rivulets that remind me how thirsty I am. If only they had a drinking fountain . . .

We stop at another room with another small table, where a man with rimless glasses making him look like an owl is sitting on a crate, smoking a cigarette. He seems to be inhaling every molecule of smoke. There's none hanging in the room, and virtually no smell.

"Hello, young man," the man says in perfect English. "Welcome."

"Thank you," I say, remembering my manners.

"Perhaps you thought you were entering Dante's Inferno, yes?" he says. "You have read this in school?"

I've heard of it but haven't read it yet. Maybe they're saving Dante for next year. "No," I say. "Sir."

He smiles. "Perhaps one day." He inhales his cigarette again, which is now hardly more than the ember. If it's burning his fingers, he doesn't show it.

"We have been waiting for you." He nods at Phuong. "To ask you some questions, that is all."

"Questions about what?" I ask, my mouth so dry I can barely get the words out.

The man picks a canteen off the floor and puts it on the table, signaling for me to drink. I don't wait for a second invitation.

"Sorenson," he says. "Your father. Tell us about him."

"We came here to visit him," I say. "But I don't know what he does or anything. Really. Just, well, that he works at the embassy."

"And what else?"

"That's all," I say. "That's all I know. He doesn't talk about what he does. Not to me."

"What has your mother told you about him?" My inquisitor isn't smiling anymore. He's all business, leaning into the table. Phuong hasn't moved since we came in. She stands by the entrance but still in my peripheral vision.

"Nothing," I say. "He travels a lot. He's been in Vietnam for, like, I don't know, three years or something. Off and on for maybe four years. We see him sometimes, and then we don't see him a lot of the time."

The inquisitor nods. "What has he said to you about his work with SOG?"

"I don't know," I say. "What's that?"

He's frowning now. I hope he isn't losing patience with me.

"Studies and Observation Group," he says, coming down hard on each word, as if to impress on me their importance. But I have no idea what he's talking about.

"I'm sorry," I say. "I really don't—"

"Your father," he interrupts. "His job is disruption."

"Disruption of what?" I ask, growing more freaked out by the second, hoping if he keeps talking he won't demand answers from me that I don't have.

"Our people call it the Reunification Trail," he says. "Your people have other names for it."

"You mean the Ho Chi Minh Trail?" I ask.

The man lights another cigarette and inhales. I don't know how he does it, but even when he exhales there isn't any smoke.

He says something to Phuong in Vietnamese, and she steps forward and takes hold of one of my arms.

To me he says, in English, "Perhaps you have nothing to say. Perhaps, as you have said, you don't know anything. Perhaps you can be of help to us, and perhaps not. We will give you time and opportunity to reflect."

He nods to Phuong and she leads me away, out of the room and farther down the same tunnel we traveled to get there. That's what I think, anyway. It's hard to say for sure, easy to get lost in this endless maze. It's like playing Chutes and Ladders, only without the board to guide you, and no wheel to spin, and everybody has guns.

We go down another ladder into another dark hole, and through yet another tunnel so dimly lit that we have to feel our way along. Phuong stops, finally, and ushers me inside a small room carved into the rock off to one side. Or maybe we're at the end of the tunnel, the end of everything. My heart races. I'm sweating, trembling, so scared I could probably pee myself again if I wasn't so dehydrated.

Two men follow us in. I don't know what happened to Vu and Trang, but it isn't them. These men pull me over to two lengths of hemp fastened to a bar bolted shoulder high to the rock wall. Phuong tells me to turn around so they can pull my arms behind me and tie my wrists to the dangling ends of the ropes, which are only long enough to allow me to stand. One of the soldiers unsheathes a combat knife. I cry out, beg him—"No! Please! Don't!"—but he only means to cut off my clothes. The shredded suit coat, slacks, paisley tie, blood-soaked dress shirt, Dad's wing tips. They even start to cut off my underwear, but Phuong says something that makes them stop.

The men step back to admire their handiwork, then they leave. Phuong leaves, too.

For a long, long time.

February 3

I don't know if you can call what happens over the next few days torture.

They don't hammer slivers of bamboo under my fingernails, or pull them off with pliers, or force me into a squatting position for hours on end, or hang me by my bound hands behind my back until my shoulders are dislocated, or scream at me, or hit me, not even with their bamboo staffs the way the guards have done on the trail when I fall and don't get up quickly, or stumble off a path, or don't move fast enough, or don't follow an order I can't understand.

They just leave me to stand, bound to the wall. I can't sit or lie down, so there's no way to rest, no way to sleep. They bring in bright lanterns and keep them blazing all the time. They bang on metal plates when my head droops and my eyes wilt shut. They shake me, throw water in my face, poke me in the ribs with their bamboo staffs, but not violently, more as if—and the very idea of it seems crazy—they're trying to tickle me into staying awake. It works.

For long periods, especially early on, they leave me to my own thoughts, which run all over the place. You can only be frightened for so long, and then something like boredom takes over when nothing happens, when it's just you by yourself and nothing to do, and no way to go anywhere or get away or get comfortable, and you're cold and getting colder unless you stomp your feet, shift from side to side, do half squats, as far as the ropes will let you, clench and unclench your fists, pull against ropes that won't give. My feet leave bloody patterns from weeping blisters, but after a while they become so caked with dirt that it looks like I'm wearing socks. I worry about infection and hypothermia and about running out of air. I worry that there might be underground snakes that will crawl on me like that white-lipped viper, that they will forget I'm here, and when they come back I'll be a cartoon skeleton, no flesh left on my bones, no organs, no tissue, no face or hair or skin, just bones, arms still bound to the wall, still standing, frozen in death.

I must start hallucinating at some point, because I'm sure Mom comes in to scold me for running off to Cholon. She scowls and says she raised me better than that, sent me to the best schools, showed me Paris, took me to all the European capitals, hired French tutors to make sure I was fluent like her, bought me whatever I needed and most of what I wanted, attended all my swim meets despite me always coming in last place, put up with Geoff even though she didn't like him, and why didn't I appreciate the sacrifices she's made and why am I such an ungrateful child and what do I have to say for myself? I shout back at her but can't understand the words coming out of my own mouth, but then I don't care because she's gone and I'm singing—all the hits of 1967: "A Whiter Shade of Pale," "Somebody to Love," "Magical Mystery Tour," "Light My Fire."

Phuong comes in, looking sad, averting her eyes from seeing me in my underwear. She lets her hair down so it hangs free around her face, and she wears an ao dai instead of her black uniform. How did I not recognized how pretty she is before? Instead of an AK-47, she carries a guitar and sings Joni Mitchell songs—in English! And here are Vu and Trang singing backup! I cry because they sound so beautiful, and they're doing it just for me.

But Dad's suddenly here in the room with me, too. Phuong and Vu and Trang vanish. They don't want to have anything to do with him, and I know he doesn't want them around. "No time for this nonsense!" he barks.

"How'd you get in here, Dad?" I ask.

"Never mind that," he says. "I'm here and I'm getting you out and you're going to enlist and we're going to win this war."

"Okay, Dad," I say. "I'll do it if you want me to. You were seventeen when you enlisted, weren't you? And you fought the Germans. You told me all about D-day, and the Battle of the Bulge. Remember your story about how the Germans surrounded the 101st Airborne in Bastogne? They demanded that you surrender or else be wiped out, but General McAulliffe wrote back his famous one-word answer—'Nuts!' I loved that story and laughed every time you told it to me. Only it wasn't just a story, it was real, and you were there, freezing in your foxhole, with trees exploding all around you and your friends under the German artillery barrage. But you didn't care. You made it sound like a party. Like General McAulliffe saying 'Nuts!' to the Germans was the thing that scared them off. So, yeah, Dad. I'll enlist. And if the North Viets ever have me surrounded and want me to surrender, I'll already have my answer ready, too: 'Nuts!' "

Dad fades. I sag, my knees buckling until my shoulders scream in pain and that wakes me. I stand, legs shaking. I lean against the stone wall and it's freezing, but I don't care. The shock of it helps keep me awake, which is a good thing, because Geoff and I decide to sneak down inside an abandoned subway tunnel deep under the city, up in the Bronx. There's a manhole cover that's come loose. A steel ladder that we climb down for, like, a mile. Water dripping off the walls. Standing puddles as big as lakes.

Our flashlights swallowed by the pitch black until we smell the fires and follow the smell and see flames leaping out of barrels and tunnel people crowded around them, warming themselves. Only the tunnel people are just homeless people—sad, ragged, homeless people—mostly old men and old women, but some younger ones, too, faces smeared with underground dirt. We've brought bags of bread, jars of peanut butter and jelly. But nothing to spread it with. They snatch it out of our hands, too hungry to thank us, I guess. It's nice that they share it with one another, though. They spread the PB&J with their fingers, but nobody cares. Geoff and I are glad to see that, and Geoff says maybe this is, like, the perfect place where everybody takes care of everybody else, the way you're supposed to. The ideal society. Except for the poverty, of course. But then suddenly we're in the glare of bright flashlights, and a whole platoon of subway cops is there, grabbing the tunnel people, grabbing our backpacks. Geoff and I wriggle free and run as fast as we can to get out of there, panicked when we can't find the steel ladder again—down to only Geoff's flashlight, which is really just one of those tiny penlights, because I must have dropped mine or one of the subway cops snatched it—but we finally run into the ladder and climb, first Geoff and then me, worried that the cops' claw hands will grab hold of my ankles and drag me back down.

I don't know when they untie me—how long it's been, whether it's day or night or something in between. I don't know when they wrap me in a blanket and lay me on the floor. I don't know when they give me water and hold me up so I can drink it, and then lay me on the floor again, and let me sleep. All those things must happen. I'm vaguely aware of the inquisitor coming in to see me, asking me more questions, saying something to other people in the room. Saying to me, from very far away but also from right next to me, "Very well. You may still be of some use to us." An echo of something he said before. I try to tell him that I'm very sorry that I disappointed him, very sorry that I can't help them.

If only I could feel my arms, or lift them higher than my shoulders. If only I could sleep some more. Just a few minutes more, really, and then I'll be ready. I promise. Ready for anything.

━━━━━━━━━━━━━━━

I don't know why the inquisitor stopped his questions, or why they freed me from the wall, and I'm too out of it to ask. Phuong and Vu and Trang get me dressed in the remnants of my suit, tying pieces of it on with bits of twine, and then they guide me out of the tunnels, up those long climbs on the wooden ladders. It's night when we emerge back into the jungle. They carry me to their camp. Phuong brings me soup with noodles and some kind of meat broth and something that looks like clumps of grass. She says it's called pho.

When I regain enough strength to sit up for any length of time, Phuong asks me the same questions as the inquisitor:

What do I know about this SOG—Studies and Observation Group? What do I know about Frank Sorenson's associates? What are their names? Where has he traveled in-country when he's not with Hanh? What has he said about Hanh? Does he suspect Hanh may be an agent for the People's Army? What has Dad told me about a spring military offensive? What has he told me about seeding clouds over the Truong Son mountains? About spotter planes with infrared capabilities? About mountaintop listening posts? About motion detectors along the Reunification Trail? About bouncing mines? About poisoned caches of rice? About automatic weapons for the Laotian mountain tribes to use against the People's Army?

"The People's Army?" I ask.

"The North Vietnamese Army," she says in French. "What you call the NVA. We call ourselves the People's Army."

I don't have answers to any of Phuong's questions—any more than I had when the inquisitor asked them in the other interrogations. Maybe this is the Vietnamese version of Good Cop/Bad Cop. Neither Phuong nor the inquisitor seems particularly bad, though. Not that any of it is good. I ask Phuong if I can go home now. It's stupid, I know. But I'm not in my right mind.

She says she's sorry, but no, that can't happen.

Later, after I fall asleep and then, hours later, wake up, she gives me more to eat—more watery pho, this time with what I'm sure are earthworms, which I know are probably a decent source of protein, but I can't make myself bite down on them or swallow them whole, so I eat around them and flip them into the brush when nobody is looking. I close my eyes and almost immediately am transported back underground, tied to that wall, forcing me to relive all those scenes of regret and desire.

The flashbacks continue for days afterward, always a shock, leaving me exhausted, spent, empty, and shaken. I have fevered dreams at night and wake up disoriented, thinking I'm still being interrogated.

February 8, morning

We're walking again, back on the narrow trail. Maybe it's a different trail than before. Maybe it's the same one. Thick brush, overhanging trees, rice paddies, dry stream beds, brutal heat. We stop outside a village and hide while Trang goes off on orders from Phuong to find new clothes for me. He comes back with black clothes and a straw conical hat, similar to what they're all wearing. The pant legs and sleeves are too short by a couple of inches but fit okay other than that, enough so that Phuong says from a distance I will look like them, and we can all pass for peasants—except for their weapons and ammo belts, and my wing tip shoes, which are still crippling my feet. I struggle with the lingering effects of sleep deprivation—everything happening in a kind of brain fog—and my aching shoulders that make it difficult to raise my arms over my head. But my feet are the worst.

I pull off the shoes to show Phuong. My toenails have turned black. The shoes are wet with fresh blood inside. She tells me I have to keep going. "We have no choice," she says. "We can't stop here, not during daylight. It's too dangerous. We must keep going."

I respond by throwing Dad's shoes into the brush.

Phuong nods to Vu and Trang, and they shove me down the trail, making me walk barefoot. Over the next few hours I seem to step on every rock, thorn, stick, and snake on the trail until I can't take it anymore. Maybe they're making me walk all the way to North Vietnam. Maybe just to the next tunnel complex, where they're planning to torture me some more. Maybe they have a secret execution site and that's where we're going. But I don't care. "I'm done!" I shout. "I can't walk." I drop to the ground in the middle of the path and refuse to get up. I even yell that I hate them. It's a pretty good tantrum. A stupid one, too.

Vu doesn't wait for orders from Phuong. He hits me hard across the shoulders with his bamboo, and then again on my thighs. I roll into a ball as he keeps hitting me until Phuong makes him stop. She drags him off into the brush and speaks to him in a loud, angry voice until he calms down. Or maybe they're just talking about the weather. From the recesses of my foggy brain it all seems abstract, even Vu beating me with his staff.

When they come back, Phuong pulls out the bamboo and noose. My heart sinks. "Okay, okay," I say in French. "You don't have to do that."

She nods and puts it away. They lift me to my feet, and once again we march—or in my case, limp—down the path. After half an hour, Phuong leads us off in a new direction, toward one of the hamlets we've been avoiding all day, except for Trang's solo excursion for clothes. I don't see it at first. The thatch-roofed huts and animal enclosures blend in with the bank of trees and brush on the far side of yet another expanse of rice paddies.

Phuong looks nervously in every direction. Vu and Trang do as well, mostly up at the clear blue cloudless sky, as if they're afraid jets will come racing over to drop bombs on our heads, or helicopters with their side-door gunners spraying everything in sight: two small boys guiding a water buffalo somewhere, women trudging toward the hamlet carrying heavy loads of something, and of course, us.

We make it safely across the rice paddies, zigzagging on the narrow dikes. Dusty-faced children blink up at us from some odd game they're playing in the dirt. Two old women, bent practically in half, squawk at Phuong and hobble away. An elderly man shows up, maybe summoned by the old women. He speaks to Phuong and Vu and Trang, then looks at me and scowls in such a way that I wonder if he might rather kill me than welcome me to his village. We follow him through the hamlet and back into the jungle. He slashes vines and thick elephant grass with his machete to make a path. It's still a struggle to keep up, until we come to a gash in the earth where trees, brush, everything has been torn violently out by their roots, or sheared and burned, or tossed by the force of impact of something that crashed there.

We follow the gash down into a ravine until we see it—the wreckage of an A-1E fighter-bomber. American. The nose and propeller are crushed and half buried, the cockpit destroyed, one wing just gone, flung somewhere I can't see. The fuselage is crumpled and partially burned, but the US Navy insignia is still visible.

"Why are we here?" I ask Phuong.

"Sandals," she says as the old man goes to work cutting rubber off one of the large, heavy tires that seem to have already been worked over in the same way before. Trang grabs my shoulder and forces me to sit, and the old man takes my foot to measure against the rubber slab. He makes his large cuts with the machete, which is disturbingly sharp, then goes to work with a smaller knife and some hemp, and in ten minutes has fashioned a pair of sandals that he gives to Phuong, who hands them to Trang, who shoves them at me to put on my feet.

They fill canteens from a nearby stream, and when they do I climb up on the side of the plane to see what's inside. The instrument panel is smashed. All the wiring has been pulled out. The seats are gone. There's no trace of the pilot. As I climb down—Vu and Trang barking at me angrily for going off without permission—I see, twenty yards away, a flight suit with the pilot's body impaled on a branch, twenty feet up, his head, hidden by helmet and visor, dropped forward to his chest, arms dangling, both legs severed. I'm furious—not just that he's dead, but that he's been left there while people from the village troop past to pirate parts from the plane.

"Can I cut him down?" I ask Phuong in French. "Can't I at least bury him?"

She shakes her head. "We have to go." And she turns, expecting me to follow. But I don't. I start walking over to the tree where the pilot hangs, until Vu and Trang catch up with me and knock me to the ground. The old man follows them. He stares hard at me for a minute. I think he's going to say something, but instead he spits a stream of black tobacco juice in my face.

They don't let me bury the pilot. I'm not sure I have the strength to do it anyway. We leave. Stumbling back down the trail. I wipe off the spit. I keep on the sandals.

━━━━━━━━━━━━━━━

We're at the outskirts, just before we get to the rice paddies, when a scrawny chicken pokes its head out of the brush. Vu snatches it and, in one quick motion, rings its neck and pulls off the head. Blood sprays out of the stump, and Vu holds the now-dead chicken upside down by its feet as the blood drains to the ground.

Phuong stops in her tracks and then explodes, shouting at Vu as he tries to back away. She points toward the hamlet, and we all march quickly back. One of the old women from before sees the dead chicken and begins yelling at Vu and Phuong.

Phuong speaks sharply again to Vu. He opens his rucksack and pulls out a small pouch and gives the old woman some coins. She stares at them, her palm open. Phuong says something else, and Vu adds to the pile. Vu and Phuong both bow to the old woman, and we leave the hamlet again—with the chicken, which I pray we'll all get to eat with the meager ration of sticky rice that evening. Something tells me it will be a long time before there's any more pho, with or without the worms.

We come up on the Saigon River the next day—Phuong tells me the name—running wide and fast. We follow the bank, coming up from the southwest, until we find a broken rock plateau that juts into the water. Phuong, Vu, and Trang squat in the brush, studying the topography. I sprawl on the jungle floor, not caring where I lie, but thankful that the back of my head finds a patch of soft moss and ferns.

Phuong sends Vu out onto the exposed rock to scout a way to cross. There's a ferry, or there was at one time, but we can see the remnants of it a short way downriver, bombed into splinters.

When Vu returns, they have a feverish conversation for a few minutes. Trang pulls a tightly coiled rope from his pack and ties it around Vu's waist. Vu doesn't look happy at all, but he doesn't say anything about having to go first. They summon me to go with them out on the rocks and help hold the rope as Vu enters the water, leaving his pack and weapon and rice pouch with us. The current sweeps him into the middle of the river. He pushes off the bottom to send himself forward, but when the water gets too deep, he dog-paddles furiously for the other side. Every time it seems as if he's making progress, he loses it to the current. But he keeps up his struggle, his wild splashing, kicking now, too, until he finally makes his way out of the current and into flat water and eventually to the other bank.

He drags himself out, catches his breath, then walks the rope up so he's directly across from us and ties the rope off to a tree near the river's edge. Trang ties our end to a boulder. He has an easier time getting across, going hand over hand, though he's carrying both his and Vu's weapons and packs. Phuong makes me go next—obviously there's no way she's leaving me alone to go last, or try to escape. I have nothing to carry except my sandals, which I'm not about to risk losing to the current.

After I make it across, Phuong unties the rope on her end, then when she plunges into the river, the current sweeps her downstream the same as it did with Vu. She holds firm to the rope with one hand and somehow manages to keep her weapon and pack over her head with the other. I can see her straining, the water up to her chin and at times over her mouth and nose. Vu and Trang give me some orders that I don't understand, until I see they're pulling on the rope to reel in Phuong to our side. I join them, and in a few minutes she's here, clearly exhausted. She lets go of the rope so she can shove her AK-47 and gear up to us on the bank.

Trang extends his hand to pull her up next, but he loses his grip, or maybe she slips. Phuong screams and then suddenly she's back in the water, sputtering, flailing, pulled away by the current.

And then under.

February 8, afternoon

Vu and Trang yell, as if she can hear them, but Phuong doesn't come back up. They're paralyzed. Maybe they can't swim. Maybe everything is just happening too fast for them to react.

Without giving it any thought, I jump in and swim after her, aiming for the spot where she went under, hoping the current will take me to her. The plunge shocks me out of the brain fog that's dogged me since the interrogation. I dive under where I think Phuong might be, but visibility is zero. I find the bottom and kick off, pushing myself farther downstream. Lungs bursting, I surface, take a breath, see an arm thrashing out of the water, and swim harder to catch up. I lift my head again. The arm is gone. I keep swimming. I dive once more and reach blindly and feel something, flesh and hair. I grab Phuong's shirt and pull her to the surface. She's limp, but I manage to get her face above the waterline. Dim memory of an old lifeguard training class that I never finished kicks in. I loop my arm under her ribs and sidestroke toward the bank, kicking out of the current, losing strength and breath with every second, too tired to keep going, but knowing I can't quit or we're both dead.

My feet touch the soft, murky bottom again, and I drag us to land. With what feels like the last of my strength, I turn her on her back, tilt her head, and do CPR, my mouth on hers, quick shallow breaths, chest compressions, whatever I can think of.

She finally shudders and coughs and vomits. I roll her onto her side so she won't choke, pull her long black hair out of her face, make sure her mouth and nose are out of the sand, and then just sit there until her breath slows to something like normal. I look around for Vu and Trang. There's no telling how far we've been pulled down the river. Another wave of fatigue sweeps over me, and I collapse in the sand next to Phuong, keeping my hand on her side to feel the shuddering rise and fall. I can't tell if she's unconscious or just exhausted to the point that she might as well be.

As long as she's breathing, though, that means she's alive. I close my eyes. I don't care if it's the middle of the day, the middle of the night, the middle of the war, the middle of anything—all I want to do is sleep.

Vu and Trang eventually find us, and we end up staying here for the night, just up the bank in a secluded spot in the dense woods, still within earshot of the murmuring river. For a long time, Phuong doesn't speak, just sits, wrapped in her poncho, back against a tree. I want to warn her about snakes, but even that seems as if it would take too much effort. I lean against my own tree but keep checking over my shoulder to make sure nothing is about to slither onto me.

Vu and Trang scowl and tend to their pots of rice and chicken—which they don't share—and some peppers they must have pilfered from the hamlet without Phuong seeing.

After they fall asleep, Phuong whispers to me in French, "Why did you save me?"

I shrug. "You were going to drown. I didn't really think about it." I'm quiet for a minute, then add, "Plus you were sort of nice to me before. I mean, you took that noose off me that first day. And in the tunnel where they tied me up, you didn't let them strip me all the way until I was, you know, naked."

"I would not have done the same for you," she says, and from the long, serious look on her face, I believe her. Almost.

"You would have died," I say. I can't think of any other reason for what I did, or why there should be another reason for saving somebody.

"Je suis votre ennemie," she says. *I am your enemy.*

"Yeah," I reply. "I guess so. Well, how about this, then: I figured I'd rather have you still be alive and in charge. I don't think

Trang likes me very much. Maybe I knew I would have a better chance of surviving with you than with him."

"Vu doesn't like you, either," Phuong says. I think maybe she'll smile when she says it, but her expression doesn't change, so she must be serious about that, too. Maybe about everything.

"This is a war, Taylor," she says, her expression still not changing. "You still don't seem to know what that means, but you will learn. I didn't know what it meant when I was a schoolgirl in the North, in Hanoi, but that was a long time ago. Before the Americans began bombing us. Before we were forced to see, right in front of us, in our own families, so much death. The carnage. Before we left our homes and came to liberate the South and face your army. You are a foolish boy who thinks he did a heroic thing. If I had died in the river, I would have died as a martyr to the great cause of uniting our country. The People's Army requires that dedication of all."

It sounds like a propaganda speech, but everything she's saying, I can tell she believes. In her mind, we're the enemy—the Americans and the South Vietnamese. And I guess the French before us. We're the bad guys. Phuong says they're fighting to liberate their own country. Geoff, whose parents are both liberal, pacifist professors at Columbia University, is always saying the same thing back home—that the South Vietnam government is corrupt, a puppet controlled by the US, and that America is on the wrong side in this war. Geoff says Ho Chi Minh is, like, the Abraham Lincoln of Vietnam, and this is their Civil War.

It's the opposite of everything I've ever heard from Dad, who says the North Vietnamese are communists, in league with the Soviet Union and the Red Chinese, out to destroy democracy. He says Ho Chi Minh is as bad as Stalin and Mao, and all the communist countries want the same thing: world domination.

I don't know what to think.

I lie back on the hard ground and close my eyes. Vu is doing a kind of whistle-snoring, until Phuong crawls over and pinches his nose. He flops around for a second and then is still. I shut my eyes again, taking some small comfort in the soft night sounds— the river, a gentle wind through the trees—and I'm almost asleep when a thought comes to me: Phuong said my name, for the first and only time. That has to mean something.

═══════════════════

The next morning it's cold sticky rice and nasty tapioca roots for breakfast—a smaller handful for me; not much more than that for Phuong, Vu, and Trang—and then we're back on our feet, following the curve of the river to find the trail we lost, or gave up, or haven't yet found after the crossing. The new sandals chafe some, but not nearly as bad as Dad's wing tips did. The black uniform I'm wearing is cooler and a lot more comfortable than what had been left of my suit, and as the sun rises and bakes the earth yet again, the straw hat is a great relief, like having an umbrella on my head to keep me in shade. Any time we find water, no matter how small the stream or how shallow the pond, Phuong, Vu, and Trang splash themselves head to toe, and then air-dry as we continue walking afterward. I start doing the same thing, and that helps keep me cooler, too.

And then suddenly there's no more jungle. We pull up short at the edge of what looks like it should be a cliff. Instead we're just a step removed from a barren landscape that stretches before us farther than we can see. A ghost forest, ground cover gone, no leaves on the trees, the trees themselves little more than white-gray stalks, thousands and thousands of them, most broken, some nothing but ragged stumps with shards so sharp that to stumble into one would mean being impaled. Everything seems white, not just the trees. Everything. Like somebody dumped massive amounts of powder in every direction.

"Qu'est-ce que c'est?" I ask Phuong. *What is this?*

"The Americans call it the Iron Triangle," Phuong says.

"What happened here?" I ask.

She scowls and then counts off on her fingers: "Phosphorus. Poison herbicide. Agent Orange. Napalm. American bombers have sprayed hundreds of thousands of kilograms across the whole province, from this forest and the Saigon River in the South, to

105

the Thi Tinh River in the East, to the Than Dien forest in the North."

"Can we go around it?" I ask. The last thing I want to do is be anywhere close to all this chemical death.

"We'll have to wait until night when we can't be seen by spotter planes or patrols," Phuong says. "And then we'll go through."

February 9, evening

We rest and sleep through the heat of the afternoon, hidden in the jungle where the air force hasn't reached with their—I guess with *our*—chemical sprays and mass defoliants and incendiary bombs.

As soon as it's dusk, we move out—Phuong once again in the lead, then Trang, me, and Vu bringing up the rear and making sure I don't try to run. Not that there's anywhere to run to. I can't see that we're following a trail anymore, so maybe it's the stars, the constellations, something nocturnal, anyway. We've only been walking for half an hour when Phuong pulls up suddenly. We all step to the side of the path. There isn't any place to hide except almost comically behind one of the white trees—all four of us. With the moon out, and no clouds, and no other cover, we couldn't be more exposed. We might as well be out in the daytime.

A line of soldiers materializes out of the ghost forest. Phuong steps out from behind the tree and quietly hails them, her voice a whisper. But the forest is so deathly quiet that it still seems to echo. The line freezes and three people in the lead, two men and a woman, separate themselves from the night army to speak to Phuong. Vu and Trang pull me out into the open as well. The officers, if that's what they are, look me over hard. One woman lifts her weapon and keeps it leveled at me.

Phuong lowers her voice even more and shows them some papers. Vu and Trang are summoned and hand over their papers as well. One of the officers produces a penlight and studies the documents, then turns the light on me, directly into my face. I blink nervously and can't stop blinking until he shuts it off.

There's more whispered conversation, and then the officers rejoin their unit and march on, or rather creep, through the prairie of dead trees and white ash. What I thought was a small unit, maybe a platoon, turns out to be several hundred—a battalion—moving not in a straight line as I also thought, but spread out much wider. We wait for them to pass, but every time I think they're gone, there's a break, and then another wave of soldiers—all of them in military uniforms, none of them with ranks showing that I can see.

And then, without warning, the night explodes. A squad of low-flying planes suddenly appears overhead, flooding the forest with searchlights. The gunships roll over on their sides as they pass, opening up with their side guns. Hundreds of rounds rain down on us, red phosphorus tracers lighting up the sky and the ground and everything in between. I know what they are—converted cargo planes that the Vietnamese call Dragon Ships because those red tracers make it look like they're spitting fire. The Americans call them Puffs, like Puff the Magic Dragon, each one capable of spewing eighteen thousand rounds a minute from three massive guns, blasting soldiers and trees into splinters. I can't move, just stand there, transfixed by the suddenness, by the awesome firepower, by the deafening sound, by the psychedelic light show, by the chaos and frenzy as everyone runs in every direction until they can't. I see a man literally shot in half not ten feet away. Two men run past me going as hard as they can, stupidly looking behind them. Both slam into trees, knocking one out completely, while the other becomes a slow-crawling target who is quickly killed, his head split open, his body dancing on the ground as more bullets catch what's left of his corpse.

My legs give out and I sit at the base of a white tree. I press my hands over my ears and, without meaning to, start shouting, not saying anything that makes sense, just noise to try to drown out the horror. The Dragon Ships keep circling and I keep squeezing, but there's no escape: It's every monster that ever hid under my bed when I was little, or lurked in my closet and sprang out at me in nightmares; it's every siren screaming toward every blood-soaked tragedy down New York streets; it's riots in Harlem, a meteor striking Earth, the atomic bomb, the end of the world.

And it stops as abruptly as it began. The Puffs straighten themselves and leave, maybe out of ammunition or maybe on to a new target, leaving behind murdered earth and skeletons of trees bursting into flame and white dust, a ghastly rain falling on everything and everybody, the living, and the dying, and the dead.

===

There's a terrible efficiency to how quickly the NVA survivors bury their dead. Teams with trenching tools hack out shallow graves. Other teams pick up bodies or what's left of them. Some collect identification papers from their dead friends, some take their weapons, some gather rucksacks and rice rations and ammo pouches and knives and anything else—uniforms, boots, helmets. Some fashion stretchers with bamboo staffs and ponchos. Others take up the stretchers and the march continues toward Saigon.

Nobody speaks to me, or gives me orders, or even seems to notice I'm here. I could be invisible.

I wonder if Phuong and Vu and Trang have been killed, and if that means I'm on my own. Free, but so far away from home that it doesn't seem possible that I could ever get back there. Not just to Saigon and the embassy, but New York. Do I even have a home anymore? My parents could be dead for all I know. The full weight of that realization—how completely and horribly alone I am in the world—makes me drop back to the ground, where I sit, legs splayed, arms so weak they fall palms up as if they'll come unattached like all those amputated limbs I carried out of the underground hospital.

Two ghosts emerge from out of the gloom—Phuong and Trang, covered in that same white dust that camouflages us all. They don't speak, just slump to the ground next to me, letting their rifles drop beside them. Nobody moves, nobody says anything, no explanation about what happened to Vu, but no need to ask. I care but I don't care. So he's dead. At least I'm not alone.

Phuong is the first to stir. She shakes herself. Lightly slaps her own face. Then says, "We can't stay here. The Dragon Ships might come back."

That doesn't seem likely, especially since the NVA battalion is long gone. There's little cover in the skeletal forest during the night, but there'll be even less during the day. So we move out, stumbling across the pocked earth. I trip a couple of times. Trang does, too, and accidentally discharges his AK-47. Phuong chews him out in Vietnamese, her voice hoarse from all the dust, or from screaming like I did during the attack, or from fatigue. Trang doesn't respond.

The Saigon River bends near us deep into our night march, the water a harsh, metallic silver. We climb down the bank to wash the dust out of our eyes and mouths, and to fill canteens. Phuong hands me the extra canteen and says to keep it. It must have been Vu's. She also gives me a rice carrier like the long cotton tubes she and Trang wear over their shoulders. She tells me it holds two weeks' worth of dried rice. I wonder if that means we're two weeks away from Hanoi, but that can't be right. From what TJ told me it would be more like two months, so we'll have to get more rice from somewhere along the way—if they're actually taking me to Hanoi. So far, Phuong hasn't said.

The sun rises that morning on a new problem: the sudden end of the trees. As dead as they were, as white and ashen, at least they broke up the landscape. But now it's as if we're walking on the moon. Even the air feels too thin to sustain us, as if most of the oxygen has been vacuumed out of this place. It's deathly quiet, our footsteps the only sounds. No birds, no forest creatures, no wind through trees, no trees at all, no wind at all, no brush, no livestock, no roads, no paths, no villages or hamlets, no people.

We pass burnt mounds of what must have once been trees and brush, but long since destroyed and turned to cinders. Then we come to the edge of an enormous crater.

Phuong stops us. The silence is so heavy that it turns just standing here into a battle with gravity.

"This was the village of Ben Suc," she says.

"It looks like a meteorite landed here," I say, looking around in horror.

"No," Phuong said. "Just Americans and South Vietnamese. They attacked from the air first and bombed every hamlet and village in this province. Then the ground troops and the tanks moved in. They dropped leaflets from spotter planes telling all who lived here that it had been declared a free-fire zone, which meant they were authorized to shoot everyone and target anything."

"There was a battle?" I ask.

"No," Phuong says. "Only a slaughter from the sky. Some escaped. Some were captured. Some were relocated. Many were killed. Afterward, they drove in with their bulldozers to destroy all the buildings, the trees, everything. More phosphorus from the air. More chemicals, not only in the village but everywhere you see. They set fires that burned for weeks."

"Because the NVA was here?" I ask.

She nods. "The National Liberation Front—the Viet Cong guerillas—had controlled the province. The North Vietnamese Army sent me and dozens of others from Hanoi to help them establish political cadres, weapons training, medical clinics. We were stationed here in Ben Suc. Until the Americans came. They found our underground stores of rice and weapons. They brought tons of explosives and placed them in bunkers under the village. Then they blew the whole village away."

She sweeps her arm in an arc in front of her. "And so the crater."

February 10

I can't get my head around how complete the devastation is, even though it's right here in front of me—like a giant mouth, silently screaming into the sky above. I've seen pictures of Hiroshima and Nagasaki after we dropped the bomb. I could at least see the remains of buildings there, the outlines of foundations and roads. Here, in the crater, there is nothing left. Nothing at all.

We follow the exposed edge of the crater, careful not to fall in. Phuong says there might still be unexploded bombs. It seems to take forever, but eventually we come to the far side and then keep going until we reach a worn path that Phuong finds, like a secret tunnel into a green forest where the devastation ends and it's the old Vietnam again—thick foliage, canopy trees, bamboo walls, tiger-tongue vines with thorns so sharp that just grazing the tips leaves bloody claw marks across my arm.

We come up on the Saigon River yet again, and Phuong lets us pause long enough to wet our bandannas and refill canteens.

"I'm sorry about Vu," I say to her, as Trang takes extra time at the river's edge. "It must be hard to lose your friend like that."

Phuong looks at me like she thinks I'm crazy. "Vu wanted to kill you," she says. "I had to threaten him to keep him from doing it. And he wasn't my friend. We were comrades, yes. But that's all."

I'm dumbfounded. "Why did he want to kill me?"

Phuong wipes her sweaty face with her damp bandanna, then ties it around her neck. It's late afternoon but still sweltering. "He didn't want to be on this mission. He wanted to join our other comrades in the battle for Saigon. He said we should shoot you and tell our superiors that you tried to escape."

"But he was always smiling," I say stupidly. "I thought he was nice. Nicer than Trang."

"Trang wanted to kill you, too," Phuong says. "He was Vu's friend, and now he wants to kill you even more. He says it's because of you that Vu is dead."

A chill shoots up my spine. I must look terrified because Phuong seems to take pity on me or something. "I won't let him," she assures me. "Unless you try to escape. But you have to do your part."

"What's my part?" I ask, trembling. "And why do you want to keep me alive, anyway?" I've come so close to being killed so many times already since getting kidnapped in Saigon, I don't know why finding this out about Vu and Trang hits me so hard. I want to throw up.

"We have our orders," she says. "You don't need to know anything else. All you need to do is your part—keep close. Don't draw attention to yourself. Don't speak to Trang. At night be still and be silent."

Trang comes up from the river and sweeps past us back onto the trail. I hesitate, then follow, keeping as much distance between us as Phuong will allow. She's close behind me, but we don't talk anymore that day. I'm tired and hungry and freaked out.

Maybe what she told me is true. Maybe it's just her way of scaring me into being compliant. But all along I've been compliant—mostly compliant, anyway—so that can't be it. I carried wounded soldiers until I thought I would pass out. Hauled amputated limbs and helped bury the dead. Walked in Dad's stupid wing tips until my feet felt like bloody stumps. Been tied to a wall in an underground dungeon until I lost touch with reality.

I haven't been any trouble, or I've tried not to be. Except for the very occasional tantrum. They have to see that. Trang has to see that.

I barely sleep that night whenever he's on guard duty. Every movement, every noise from his direction, hidden near us in the woods, I tense up, my eyes shoot open, and it's all I can do to keep from scrambling into the brush so he can't kill me while Phuong is asleep.

We skip breakfast the next morning, Phuong wanting to put more distance between us and the ghost forest and Ben Suc. Early that afternoon, the jungle path opens onto a wide expanse of elephant grass, half a mile across, and we wade through, following what appears to be the intended trail, judging from some of the grass that's bent and in some places trampled, as if a group of people congregated in those places, then resumed snaking through in single file.

One minute Trang is in front of me, and the next minute I'm lying facedown with a loud buzzing in my ears, my eyes clouded over, blood covering my face and hands and everywhere else. Phuong is standing over me, speaking but not making any sound. I try to ask her, "What? What?" But nothing. I check my face for wounds. Then I check my arms and legs and torso. All that blood, but none of it seems to be mine.

"Trang," Phuong is saying. "It was Trang."

I sit, my head spinning. I hold it with both of my bloody hands. That stops the spinning. Some. I wipe the blood off on elephant grass. I start to get up, but Phuong grabs my arm and holds me in place. "Trang," she says again.

"What?" My brain isn't working right. My mouth isn't working right.

She points and I see: what's left of him, which isn't much. It's Trang's blood on me. Trang's guts. I grab more elephant grass and rub as hard as I can to make it go away. It won't. Not all of it. Not enough.

Phuong takes my arm again and shows me what she wants me to do. Back out, retrace our footsteps, don't step anywhere we didn't step before on the way in.

"C'était une mine," she says. *It was a mine.*

I follow her. Her voice sounds very far away though she's still holding onto my arm. Trang had been right in front of me. Trang stepped on a mine. Trang is dead now, too. I tell myself these things. I think about what would have happened if Phuong had been in the lead. And what Trang would have done to me afterward. Or what if I had been the one in the front?

We're back in the jungle, safe but not safe, because nowhere in Vietnam is safe. Death waits around every bend. Death is never more than a footstep away. Death doesn't even wait. Death hunts you down. Death comes for you in a thousand ways. I could have been killed days ago, not by American bombs or Vietnamese soldiers or Dragon Ships in the night. I could have drowned in the Saigon River. I could have been murdered by a white-lipped viper. I break down, and Phuong, who has hardly changed expression the whole time I've been with her, breaks down, too.

═══════════════════════

There won't be any burying Trang. After five minutes, maybe ten, Phuong composes herself, stands up, shoulders her rucksack and rice carrier, grabs her AK-47, and we leave, circling the meadow, keeping inside the tree line, though it's slow going as we wade through dense thickets or find ourselves blocked by stands of bamboo. Phuong's machete is useless there, but she keeps it out for hacking through lighter brush.

We come across a stream, maybe a tributary to the Saigon River, though we haven't seen it since the day before as we began heading north. Phuong looks at me and looks at herself. We're both still caked in Trang's blood. She points to a pool and tells me I can bathe in there, and I should wash out my clothes.

"What about you?" I ask.

"I'll be close by."

Phuong disappears around a bend in the stream. Once she's out of sight, I sink into the pool, sandals and clothes and all, though the water barely covers me when I lie down. I rub on my pants and shirt, and the water turns red, but the stains are still there, so I peel off my clothes and scour away the blood using fistfuls of mud. I rub it in my hair, over my face, down my arms, ducking under the water again and again, like I'm in a washing machine.

Afterward, I collapse in soft grass with my clothes spread out next to me where the sunlight breaks through the canopy. I feel clean, or something like it, for the first time since Saigon, nearly two weeks before. My ribs stand out like marimba bars, a sign of how little I've been eating, and how much weight I've lost. I can feel every bone in my body. My stomach is concave.

But at least I'm no longer wearing another man's blood.

February 11

I wake up alone. Still daylight, but the sun has shifted. Ants are crawling on my face and arms and chest, but not biting. Maybe there isn't enough of me left for them to bother. I brush them off and sit up. My clothes are damp—they haven't dried much at all—but I pull them on anyway. The bloody water has all washed downstream, so I fill the canteen and pick up Vu's rice pouch.

I step through trees and brush to find Phuong asleep on her back in her own patch of soft grass around a bend in the stream. She has on a thin undershirt and shorts, and is cradling her weapon. Her black uniform is spread on the ground. I watch her for a while, not sure if I should wake her—or if this is my chance to escape. What if I slip over and grab the AK-47? Her machete is lashed onto her rucksack, and I could get to that, too. I could get to everything.

But I'm too afraid. Too lost. Too helpless. And besides, it was Vu and Trang who wanted to kill me, not Phuong. She protected me from them. But for what? To take me to the Hanoi Hilton? Or someplace between here and there—someplace even worse?

She stirs, making the decision for me—not that there was really a decision to make. She rubs her eyes and slowly sits. Her long black hair hangs loose down her back. She sweeps it from her face, combs her fingers through to ease out tangles, and then lets the hair cascade down her back again. Her face is softer than before. Maybe relaxed from sleep. But no. Her expression changes. Tears stream down her cheeks again. She doesn't bother to wipe them.

She pulls her weapon closer, pushes the stock into the earth between her knees, and presses her forehead against the barrel, as if she's praying. I retreat to my side of the green wall of brush. Back to my side of the war. Leaving Phuong to hers for a while longer. I feel like a voyeur. I guess I *am* a voyeur. Not that she was doing anything, or that there was anything to see. Just a girl with a gun, crying.

━━━━━━━━━━━━━━━

That day we walk deep into twilight. After the deathlike silence of the ghost forest and the Ben Suc crater, the chattering of insects and birds and monkeys and other night creatures is deafening. Phuong finds a path for us to follow, but I wonder if it's the right one, whatever that might be, and wherever it's supposed to take us.

She makes me walk in front, and whenever I'm uncertain about direction in those places where the trail is faint, or branches off from itself, or seems to stop altogether, she gives me instructions in her careful French. But those are the only times she speaks the rest of the day. I'm too busy staring at the trail in front of me, desperately looking for signs of another land mine, to think about much of anything else, which is both a mercy and a curse. My stomach is knotted with fear. Once, after I run out of water and don't hydrate for a couple of sweaty hours, I grab my knees and bend over, dry-heaving.

It finally gets too dark for even Phuong to continue, so we set up camp—which consists of nothing more than her boiling the last of her water to make sticky rice and cook the remaining tapioca root. I'm so thirsty that I can barely swallow my share.

Phuong assures me that we'll have plenty of water the next day. Or perhaps the day after that.

"When we cross into Cambodia," she adds, as if that's an afterthought and no big deal.

"So we won't be in Vietnam anymore?" I ask.

"Not for some time," she says.

The forest is quiet, the night black. A faint breeze whispers in the branches overhead.

"Will you tell me where we're going?" I ask. "Where you're taking me?"

"North," she says. "That's all I can say."

I press her further. "To North Vietnam? To Hanoi?"

She doesn't answer.

"I was told there's a prison there, where they put Americans. They call it the Hanoi Hilton. They torture Americans." My voice is shaky as I say this. I want her to tell me it isn't true, even if I know I won't believe her.

Instead she changes the subject. Sort of. "In the South, there is an island, Con Son Island, just off the coast. It was once a French prison. Now the Americans and the South Vietnam government hold prisoners there in tiger cages."

She doesn't wait for me to ask about the cages before explaining. "They're under the ground, only half as tall as a person. The floors and walls are stone. The ceilings are iron bars, where guards walk. They feed the prisoners from there. They do other things to the prisoners from there as well—you can probably imagine what. The prisoners can't stand, or walk, or exercise. If they're ever released, they can no longer walk. Their muscles in their legs have atrophied, leaving them crippled." She pauses. "We have heard from many people who have been imprisoned at Con Son that this isn't all they do there."

I think about the days the inquisitor kept me tied to the wall in the tunnels, starved me, broke me.

"Is that what they do in Hanoi, too?" I ask. "For revenge?"

"I don't know," she says. "In war, it's not okay to use torture."

"But they do," I respond. "Right? Both sides? It's all terrible, no matter who you're fighting for, or why you're fighting?"

They aren't really questions.

"It's war," Phuong answers.

―――――――――――――

She ties me to a tree that night, even though I promise I won't go anywhere or try to escape. And even though she left me alone on the bank of that creek after Trang was killed. "There's no one to keep watch," she says. "You could try to steal my weapon."

"But I wouldn't," I say.

"But you might," she replies.

Hours later, something wakes me. Phuong shouting in her sleep. She thrashes on the ground, trying to free herself from the tangle of poncho wrapped around her legs. She sits up suddenly and holds her head in her hands.

"As-tu eu le cauchemar?" I ask her. *Did you have a nightmare?*

She nods and keeps pressing her hands against her temples, as if to squeeze out the memory of it, or maybe stop the disorientation that always comes after, at least for me.

I ask if she's okay. "Est-ce que tu vas bien?"

She whispers back a faint, "Oui."

My hands are bound behind my back, with another rope threaded behind my elbows and tied around the tree—just like

126

that first night outside the underground hospital with the other prisoners.

I don't want to feel bad for Phuong, but I can't help it, either, and if I wasn't restrained, I would probably go over and sit next to her. I do what I think is the next best thing—offer to stay awake and talk, until she feels like sleeping again. She says she would like that.

At first it's twenty questions. I ask Phuong how old she is, where she's from, how she learned French, if she volunteered to go to Ben Suc.

"I'm eighteen," she says, which surprises me. I knew she was young, but not *that* young. I lie and tell her I'm eighteen, too, but she looks skeptical.

"I already told you I'm a city girl, from Hanoi," she says. "My mother and father were both pharmacists. They wanted me to attend pharmacy school as well. But they understood that I was needed in the fight to unify Vietnam. Everyone was needed. Also, my volunteering to travel to the South, to live here and fight, is a way to prove to Communist Party officials that I can be trusted, and that my family can be trusted."

"I don't understand," I say. "Why wouldn't they trust you or whatever?"

"Because we aren't from the working class, like the peasants, and factory workers, and farmers. So my family—my parents and my four brothers and sisters and myself—were treated with some suspicion. That's the case with many who were from the professional class when Vietnam was a colony of France, especially if they were trained in Europe and not at schools in Hanoi. My parents had studied in Paris."

She pauses, then adds, "But now I'm committed to the resistance, and to the cause of reunification. We all are. My family. Everyone in the North. And many in the South."

I like hearing her voice, disembodied as the night grows even darker until we're no longer ourselves, or no longer our full selves, but just our voices, just our stories.

"So do you have, like, a boyfriend?" I ask.

She laughs. "No," she says. "Not anymore, since I was in school. And do you have a girlfriend?"

I think about that girl Beth, but she seems so far away, not just in distance, because it must be a lifetime ago that I met her in the Village at that psychedelic concert. I can't even summon up an image of her face anymore.

"No," I say. "Well, kind of, yes. I mean, no, not really."

"You sound confused," she says. "Do you *know* what a girlfriend is?"

"Of course," I say. "It's just that I haven't known her very long. And now I'm here. And she probably forgot all about me by now."

"I understand," Phuong says, though I can't read her tone. "In

Vietnam, once you're no longer a schoolgirl, you would never be alone with a boy, or with a young man. You would have to have your family give permission even for the young man to visit your home—after your parents have met the boy's family, of course."

"What about this?" I ask. "You and me, here. What would they think?"

"They would understand that you are a prisoner," Phuong says, "and that I have my orders to follow. And they would understand that I was supposed to have two comrades with me, to escort the prisoner. They would also understand that in war, you or your comrades can be killed in a thousand ways, that they can be with you one minute, and then in the next minute . . ."

She doesn't finish, and I don't ask her to. I picture her and Trang, covered in dust and blood after the Dragon Ships' murderous assault in the ghost forest—without Vu. I picture Trang, or what was left of him, in the flattened elephant grass after stepping on the land mine. I wonder if it's like this for everybody in war: You remember the terrible things nobody should ever have to see, but the longer you're in it, the more you start to forget everything that was normal and good.

The night silence creeps back in.

February 13

The next two days we travel hard, keeping to the forest as much as possible but having to venture out under the brutal sun to cross miles of rice paddies with no shelter or shade, except the occasional copse of trees where the dikes converge to make small islands, or when we stumble on tiny hamlets where the children hide once they see strangers approaching, and especially when they realize one of them is an American. We can't drink the stagnant water in the rice paddies, but we find a couple of dirty streams along the way and make do.

Sometimes Phuong stops abruptly and listens for the telltale drone of a spotter plane. Twice, when she hears something, we dive into the nasty water and hug the bank until the plane circles and leaves, then we scramble back onto the dike and run for cover in case it comes back, which she says happens a lot—an old trick to coax NVA soldiers out of hiding. I have to fight back the impulse to stand up on the dike and yell and wave and throw off my straw hat and show them my American face.

But she's still the one with the AK-47, and I'm still her prisoner. Even if we're lying facedown in the rice paddies together.

Sometimes we talk, other times we don't.

At one small village, a farmer has just slaughtered a pig. It's hanging upside down, the blood from its slit throat draining into a bucket. There was a time when I would have been grossed out seeing that, but now I don't think anything about it at all. Phuong offers to buy some of the meat, but the farmer insists on giving us some, maybe seeing how thin and hungry we both are, or maybe he's just afraid of Phuong's gun.

That night we have a feast—not only the roasted pork, but some bean sprouts and peppers the villagers also share with us. I nearly cry as fat from the pork drips off into the fire while we turn it on a homemade spit. What a waste! We probably don't wait long enough for it to cook all the way through before we pull the meat off the bone.

Phuong chews everything slowly, thoughtfully, as if it's just another meal rather than the first real food she's had in a week. I shove my mouth into my bowl to lick it clean.

She cuts me off when I reach for a second helping. "Enough. We save the rest for tomorrow."

I know she's right, that we shouldn't eat it all at once, but I still would steal every bite if I could get away with it.

To distract myself I say, "How did the pilots of those Dragon Ships know about the NVA battalion crossing the ghost forest? Like, the exact time and place."

"I doubt it was spotter planes," she says. "But there are other ways they have of finding our troop locations. The Americans have put censors, thousands of them, in places where they think we'll be traveling. Or it could have been the work of spies. We've discovered secret transmitters hidden near the Trail. You remember the questions you were asked about your father. We suspect that he, or others he works with, are behind much of this surveillance."

I wish I could ask my dad about it myself. It all sounds so complicated and technical—and sinister. Almost like a game, like if pinball and chess got married and had a kid, and they armed that kid with the most lethal weapons on the planet.

"Of course there's also the element of luck. Or bad luck," Phuong says. "Often the censors don't work correctly. Once the Americans slaughtered a herd of elephants in a bombing raid in Laos. I've heard that sometimes they pick up sounds of the wind in the trees, and the trees swaying. Sometimes they have targeted montagnards, the mountain people who live near the Trail. Many of them have been killed as well."

"How do you know so much about the Trail?" I ask.

"You're not the first prisoner I've been assigned to escort on the trails," she says. "I've been here before, and much farther north as well. I had experienced guides with me the first time, and the second time. Then I became the experienced one."

"Have you gone farther north than Cambodia?" I ask, hoping to get her to confirm where we're going.

"Only once, into Laos," she says.

"What about to Hanoi?" I ask.

She shakes her head. "No. Any prisoner being taken that far, I was ordered to hand off to others at one of the supply stations in Cambodia or Laos."

"What about this time, with me?"

She hesitates. "We're never supposed to tell prisoners this information. But . . ." She hesitates again. She doesn't finish. But now I'm more convinced than ever that our ultimate destination is Hanoi. And my heart sinks at the thought of it.

Much later, we're resting by a shaded stream after hours of walking that started before sunrise. The buzz and whir of insects keeps us company; we haven't seen another human since yesterday. I ask Phuong about Ben Suc—how she managed to survive when so many others didn't.

"We knew that the Americans were coming," she says. "So in some ways we were able to prepare. But we could only prepare so much. Cadres were sent to Cambodia before the American attack. Teams spread out deep into the countryside. But many of us were still in the village when the bomb and the rocket attacks started. There were helicopters, gunships, and fighter-bombers. We recognized the scream of the jets, dropping bombs and spraying automatic weapons fire on Ben Suc.

"After that came the heavy artillery, bombarding us once they were able to draw close enough after the aerial assault. They destroyed most of our supplies and many of our bases. But they didn't find all our leaders when the American troops and the ARVN swept through and began the arrests. Some fled, some hid, some stayed and fought and died, some perished before there was anyone to fight, only death from the sky. I was able to escape and make my way to the Saigon River, where I covered myself with mud and held on to roots to stay hidden along the banks. That was where I met Vu and Trang. We hid for three days, only able to come out in the dark. But with so many Americans in the area we couldn't go far to look for food, and we had to hide ourselves again during the day.

"The second night at the river another comrade found us, just before dawn," she continues. "He slid down the bank and would have gone into the water if we hadn't caught him. He had been wounded. An awful injury to his shoulder—his arm was only barely hanging on. There was so much blood. He was incoherent, mumbling, weeping. We did all we could. We pressed mud into his wound, made a poultice with grasses from the riverbank, kept pressure on to try to staunch the flow of blood.

"But he was in so much pain. He begged me to help him, to take him to his family. He was feverish. He became agitated. And louder. Vu and Trang and I tried everything to help him, but it became clear that if he stayed with us he would give away our position. The Americans would find us, and they would kill us all.

"When he began shouting, we had to do something. Trang pressed his hand over the man's mouth to quiet him, but he wouldn't be quieted. He struggled against Trang, clawed at him. Vu said we had to push him out into the current and let the river take him. We had already seen bloated corpses, many of our comrades, men and women, float past us. It was a river of death. But Trang said the man would panic more and give us away, and it would be a more terrible death for him to drown.

"So Vu and Trang held him, turned him over, and forced his face deep into the mud. I held his legs. It was all I could do. I was so ashamed. We didn't even know his name. Trang lay on top of the man. Vu kept his hand on the back of the man's head, pressing it down hard, so he couldn't breathe."

She draws a deep breath of her own, then lets it out. "It didn't take long."

I think that's the end of her story, but she isn't finished. She says, "We eased his body into the water and set him free."

February 15

We're lost, though Phuong won't say so. But I can tell. She takes us down jungle trails that dead-end into hostile brush. She slashes our way through with her machete, or as far as we can get before she drops to the ground to rest, her face dripping with sweat, barely able to lift her arm from exhaustion. Once, sitting splay-legged on the jungle floor, she lets a viper slither close, inches from her feet. She doesn't move. Even when I reach for the machete and slice off the viper's head. She gives me a dead stare, lifts her canteen to her lips, then holds out her hand. I give her back the machete.

"Are we lost?" I ask, but she says no, just orienting ourselves, whatever that's supposed to mean.

"Soon we'll arrive at a training and supply camp," she says. "Deep in the jungle—hard to find even for those who know it's there, which means it's impossible for the Americans to find."

We keep hiking, all that day and into the next, but there's no sign of the camp. I don't say anything, though. I just go where she tells me, rest when she tells me, and try not to think about home and where I'm going instead, farther and farther away.

I didn't know what to say when she told me about her and Vu and Trang and what happened to the man on the banks of the Saigon River, and I still don't know what to say. It's so far outside my experience—at least my experience before the night of Tet. A part of me keeps repeating that it can't be true. No one would ever do anything like that to anybody else.

But of course it's true. The murders of the MPs, the night of the executions, the underground hospital, the body parts in the jungle, the malaria victims in the tunnels, the shredded victims of the Dragon Ships in the ghost forest, Trang's gore—after all that, how can I not believe that Phuong and Vu and Trang killed a wounded man in his delirium, smothered him in the muddy bank of the Saigon River?

But what do I have to say back to Phuong? "That's terrible"? "How awful for you"? "I'm so sorry"?

Do I tell her about my misdeeds in New York—shoplifting records from a music store and getting chased down the street, jumping turnstiles to ride the subway for free, sneaking out to clubs in the Village, cheating on tests at Dalton, that time Geoff and I climbed underneath New York in search of the tunnel people?

But that all seems so lame, doesn't it? Compared to Phuong's life and all she's had to do, all she's had to endure.

━━━━━━━━━━━━━━━━━━━━━━━━━━━━━

We're clearly in the foothills of something. Instead of the flat, sprawling acres of rice paddies and dense stands of bamboo that can hide a company of soldiers, we find ourselves on narrow trails crowded by unbroken forest, and climbing and then descending rolling hills and then up steeper slopes, wading deeper and deeper into more hostile vegetation. More tiger-tongue vines. Ridiculously tall palms. Twice coconuts shake loose and fall— landing with a loud thud just a few feet from where we're walking. If they'd hit us, we'd be dead.

At least it gives us something to eat.

As if all that isn't bad enough, I wake up the next morning with a white rash on my arms that itches like mad. But when I scratch it, white splotches spread farther up my arms, as if whatever is under my skin is trying to get away from the scratching. It spreads all over my torso and legs as well. And worse, my face swells so bad I can't swallow. My cheeks get so puffy that I can barely see.

I'm stumbling over every rock, every hole, every vine on the trail, when Phuong comes to an abrupt halt. There are people, some in pants and shirts, some only half-dressed. A couple of them have rifles, but others carry spears, bows, knives. It's like something out of one of those old war movies I saw with my dad years ago where the landscape is empty and then the enemy is just suddenly there.

Phuong tries to speak with them, but they don't know Vietnamese, and she doesn't know whatever language they speak. There's a lot of pantomiming, some flashing of money. I'm so miserable, still clawing away, continuing to spread the white cloud under my skin, that I think about grabbing Phuong's machete and scraping the blade wherever I itch, which by now is everywhere.

Phuong tells me to follow them, and she shoves me in their direction, off the trail we've been blundering down and onto another that could be mistaken for nothing more than a random break in the bamboo.

We don't go far before the jungle opens into a clearing with a dozen thatch-roofed huts, a couple of open fire pits, children dancing around us and pointing and laughing, elderly women wearing some sort of sarong or skirt, some bracelets, necklaces, but little else, squatting close to the fires, tending to things cooking.

Someone grabs me by the arm and pulls me down on a grass mat under one of the huts. Phuong takes my empty rice sash and canteen and hat, then tells me to take off my shirt and pants.

"They will need to boil your clothes," she says. "You must have laid in a patch of something. I don't know what they say it is, but it's causing your rash."

The itching is so bad that I don't care about being left in my underwear. I balk when two women come at me with fists full of leaves, but they grab my arms and start rubbing the leaves all over me, head to toe, painting me with something sticky. It smells terrible, but the relief is immediate. "Thank you!" I gush, not sure if they understand. They smile at each other and keep rubbing, a second round, and then a third. I could cry, it feels so good to not feel so miserable anymore. With every breath I take, the itching subsides more, and after maybe an hour, the rash is all but gone. The women leave me sprawled on the mat, relieved, spent, done.

Phuong comes to check on me after a while. She has my clothes, which are steaming and still wet. I don't put them on right away. She also has a bowl of food, a stew of some kind. It smells nearly as bad as the leaf resin the women rubbed on me, but that cured the itching, so who am I to complain? My stomach growls, telling me to just eat it already.

I drink and chew and force myself to swallow the chunks of unfamiliar meat. It's so tough that I could chew for an hour and not break it down, so I just swallow and keep eating until it's gone.

"What was that?" I ask Phuong when I finish.

"You may not want to know," she says.

"No really," I insist, though from the way she says it, she might be right.

"Singe," she says. She makes a simian face and bends her elbows to tickle herself under both armpits, in case I don't know the French word for monkey.

I think I'm going to throw up. Phuong points to a skinned carcass hanging on a rack just out of the reach of a few skinny dogs. It looks almost human—dead human with most of the flesh stripped off.

"Why didn't you tell me before?" I ask.

She shrugs. "Because you wouldn't have eaten it," she says. "But it's necessary. We have to continue and you need food for strength. I doubt there will be more coconuts on the Trail. And we have no more rice."

"But *monkey*?" I'm still struggling to keep from losing it.

"These people are hungry themselves," Phuong says. "They may be starving. Many of my people making their way on the Reunification Trail are starving. The Americans have disrupted everything with their bombing raids, their mass destruction anywhere they suspect we may be. In Vietnam, in Cambodia, in Laos. Crops, livestock, the wild animals these people hunt to feed themselves. All killed. And you complain about eating monkey.

Do you not realize they are sharing with us all they have for themselves?"

Embarrassed, I start to apologize—which isn't something I'm used to—but Phuong cuts me off.

"Next time you will go without," she says.

"Can we at least stay here for the night?" I ask, but she says no, we've already lost too much time and have to get farther down the trail before stopping for the night. She doesn't know the name of the tribespeople but does her best to thank them for the food and for treating my rash. She offers them the money that apparently they hadn't accepted when she showed it to them before, but they just look at it, then drop it on the ground as if it's nothing.

We shouldn't have eaten the monkey.

I find out first, an hour down the trail, when I'm hit by stomach cramps. I try to ignore them at first—I've had dysentery off and on since Saigon—but when they get too bad, I double over, drop to my knees, and vomit up everything I've eaten.

Five minutes later, Phuong is on the ground next to me, throwing up so hard that she ends up on her hands and knees, her AK-47 flung to the side. It's noisy and nasty and violent and terrible in every way. My stomach is on fire. Phuong rolls onto her side and curls up in a fetal position, arms crossed over her abdomen, rocking and moaning.

I know we can't stay here, exposed, so I crawl off the trail, pulling her with me, until we find our way into a stand of bamboo and enough space for a nest where we can collapse, hidden, until hopefully the monkey, whatever of it is still in our bodies, somehow can pass through without killing us.

February 16

Both of us vomit over and over, deep into the night, until nothing comes out, then we dry-heave. I spit up blood. Drink some water, but as soon as it hits my stomach the vomiting starts all over again. The same with Phuong. After, we both collapse back on the ground. And then come the chills. And the delirium. It goes on for hours, and must be going on with Phuong, too, but I'm too weak, too helpless to check. Everything aches. I'm freezing. Each breath causes muscle spasms. I see things, hear things: people whispering on the other side of the bamboo, Vietnamese voices, conspiring to attack us. They have machetes. They're going to hack us to death, and no one will know. I try to warn Phuong, but I can't find her. I search for her, back in the ghost forest, going from white tree to white tree, fearful of who might be hiding behind each one, but compelled to find out, to keep on until I reach her. There's Vu, alive again, but faceless, mute, uncomprehending when I speak to him, walking blindly, arms extended, trying to feel his way somewhere. And my mom! She's there! I call to her, but she doesn't answer. I run to catch up, but she keeps moving away from me, and no matter how fast I run, I can't make up the distance. "Mom! Mom!" I scream in desperation. I have to catch her. We have to find a way home. But someone is moaning close by. It's Phuong and she needs me. I have to let Mom go.

My fever breaks. The delirium passes. I'm bathed in sweat, my face pressed to the damp ground, grit in my mouth, a desperate thirst, night so black I can't see anything. I feel around me until I find a canteen. I drink until it's empty. A voice says, *Go easy, go easy, you'll make yourself sick again*, but I can't stop. I lie back down, sweat rolling off my face, my clothes soaked, but at least the nausea is gone, along with the chills and the hallucinations. Black turns gray, and when I force my eyes open I can make out shapes. The bamboo walls surrounding us. Phuong, her back to me, still shaking and whimpering. I find her rucksack, pull out her poncho, and drag it over her, but she's thrashing now and throws it off. I gather it over her again, and this time wrap my arms around her and hold on.

And little by little it works. She stops shaking. I stop sweating. And I keep my body pressed against hers, both of us curled up together on the jungle floor, and merciful sleep comes and that's how we survive the night.

In the morning, while Phuong still sleeps, I pull myself away from her and stagger out of the bamboo with the canteens in search of more water. Amber light filters through the thick canopy, and all the voices of the jungle seem to waken at once—the birds, the monkeys high in the trees, barking deer. Every step is a chore as I follow the trail up what should be a gentle rise, hoping I'll find a stream soon. I don't have the strength to go far. I stop and listen for the sound of running water, and after two false leads, I hear it for real. Not more than a trickle, but enough to fill the canteens until my knees start trembling and my legs threaten to give out. It's too much, too soon. I have to crawl back to the bamboo nest and Phuong.

She's still passed out. I lift her head and gently pour water onto her chapped lips. She swallows. I let her rest, then do it again. I brush her long black hair out of her face, use some of the water to wash off vomit and dirt, let her sleep, and lie down to sleep again myself. I don't know why I'm working so hard to save her. It's just what you do. But also, if she dies, I die. I have no idea where I am in this jungle and can't possibly survive out here on my own. What are the chances of my being rescued on the Trail? I'm more likely to be killed by American bombs.

When I wake the second time, Phuong is the one sitting, leaning against the bamboo, her legs drawn up in front of her, forehead on her knees. She hears me struggle to sit as well and lifts her head and gives me a wan smile. The effort of even that seems to exhaust her. She puts her head back down. I drink some water, nudge her arm with the canteen. She drinks some, too.

The next hour passes in that way—one of us remembering to drink, then reminding the other to do it, too, slowly rehydrating, slowly coming back to ourselves. The morning turns into late morning, judging from the angle of the sun's rays that find their way into our hiding place. It grows warmer, but not as bad as the fierce January heat back on the plains of Vietnam. Just almost as bad. Phuong hasn't spoken all morning. Neither of us has. Neither of us do. Neither of us has the strength. Maybe neither of us has anything to say.

I crawl out again for more water and manage to stand longer this time to fill the canteens. Then I drag myself back to the bamboo. Phuong has retrieved her weapon, rucksack, and gear. It's all next to her now, the gun across her lap. She might have even cleaned it. So if she needs to shoot me, or shoot anybody, she'll be ready. It makes me angry, or as angry as I can get in my weakened state. Here I am getting water for her, after holding her all night through her chills and fever sweats and everything, and all she can think about is her gun, which means all she thinks about me is that I'm still her prisoner. So maybe I should have taken the weapon in the middle of the night, once my fever passed, and just gone ahead and shot her instead. Too bad I don't know how to fire the thing.

I throw her canteen to the ground next to her, but she catches it and looks up at me, surprised.

"Merci, Taylor," she croaks, the first and only words either of us have spoken. And for some reason that makes me feel better. I guess my emotions are all over the place—from being so sick, from being so weak, from being so starved, from everything that's happened over the past two weeks, from having my world be upside down with no chance of it ever being right again.

"Pas de tout, Phuong," I say back, because even with all that I guess I should still be polite. *Not at all.*

We rest, refill canteens, rest some more. Sleep again that night in our little fortress, though Phuong says we need to be careful about bamboo pit vipers, which scares me enough that it's hours after she dozes off before I quit worrying enough to fall asleep, too.

We both wake before dawn when it's too dark to venture out. I only know Phuong is awake because I can just make out the shape of her sitting up, and because I can hear her talking softly to herself, her voice barely a whisper. I listen for a while and realize she's singing. So I lie there, keeping still and enjoying the sound, though I don't know any of the words.

Finally, at first light, she stops. We drink the last of our water.

"We should continue today," Phuong says. "We're perhaps two days' walk from the supply base. We might run into NVA patrols. We should meet up with a wider trail, maybe by tomorrow, wide enough for truck convoys. Hopefully we'll be able to find food soon."

She checks her gear, repacks her rucksack, and picks up her AK-47.

I ask her a question that's been weighing on me since I learned about the attack on the embassy.

"Phuong, do you know if my parents are alive?"

She looks at me evenly, her face drawn.

"Back in Saigon," I add, "they were at the embassy when your soldiers attacked."

"I don't know," Phuong says. "I wasn't there. But perhaps you can tell me if *my* mother is alive. My father as well. And my sisters and little brother."

"What do you mean?" I ask. "How would I know anything like that?"

"The Americans have been dropping bombs on Hanoi for years, thousands and thousands of bombs. I haven't had any letters from my family in more than a year. Since before Ben Suc. You think I may know something about the fate of your mother, so maybe you know something about the fate of my family." She sounds angry. "They are your bombers, after all, dropping your bombs. The Americans say they only target military installations, but that's a lie. Many civilians are killed—children, parents, elderly people."

I want to protest that those weren't *my* bombing raids. I'm an American, but nobody asked my permission to bomb Hanoi, or anywhere else. And my mom is a civilian, too, and has nothing to do with the war. And my dad—Phuong seems to know more about him than I do, and I don't know what to believe. What if he is the one responsible for bombing the Trail? Does that make me guilty, too? Or is guilt even the right word when you're doing what your country tells you to do, no matter whether it's right or wrong? No matter whether you're my dad or Phuong.

All those questions from the inquisitor, and from her, all the things I've been told, about Dad and the not-so-secret war in Laos and Cambodia to destroy the Ho Chi Minh Trail. She wants answers, or confirmation, or details. I guess I want those, too. But mostly I just want Mom and Dad to be alive, and safe. And I want to be alive and safe and with them again.

February 18

The aftermath of the rancid monkey stew leaves us depleted. We struggle down the trail, but every few hundred steps, one or the other of us has to sit and rest. At the rate we're going, I guess it will take a week, not a day, to get to that wider trail Phuong promised—and to the possibility of finding an NVA convoy.

Neither of us is hungry, but Phuong says we have to eat anyway, or we'll never have the strength to make it. Only we're out of food. So she sets her AK-47 on single-shot and kills a barking deer. It happens as we sit yet again on the ground, exhausted from our last hundred meters, so wiped out neither of us moves for several minutes, even when insects buzz our faces, drawn to the streaming sweat. Three small antlerless deer wander up the path toward us, downwind and oblivious, until Phuong aims the gun. The deer barks and the blast are simultaneous. Two flee, one doesn't, its head torn almost entirely off its body by the force of the shot. Phuong and I approach cautiously, as if it might spring back to life.

I think the deer will be larger, but as we draw close, the opposite happens. I can't believe how small it is, maybe the size of a baby goat. There can't be much meat.

"I haven't done this before," Phuong says. I don't know whether she means firing her gun or killing barking deer. Though I'm betting on the deer.

"Do you know how to clean it?" I ask. "Take off the hide. Cut out the organs. All of that?"

"No," she says. "Do you?"

I shake my head. "I grew up in New York City," I say. "There aren't any barking deer in New York, unless they're in the zoo. And you're not supposed to shoot things at the zoo."

"I also grew up in the city," Phuong reminds me, sounding slightly annoyed.

Since neither of us know what we are doing, we butcher the deer together, taking turns with Phuong's combat knife hacking away the hide and the white stuff underneath that keeps it attached to the meat. I'm so grossed out that I know I would start throwing up again if I had anything left inside me. Phuong keeps having to turn away from the butchering. I slit open the deer's belly and all kinds of disgusting entrails and organs and blood and other fluids pour out, attracting an even bigger swarm of flies. We keep hacking away, separating as much as we can of what seems edible from what doesn't. When we're done, we throw everything

153

we aren't keeping off the trail, figuring the flies will take half and night creatures will drag away the rest.

At the next stream we stop with our load, start a fire, and fashion a spit, trimming the bark off a small branch and spearing as many pieces of meat as will fit, then propping it over the flames. The meat quickly blackens. The fire pops and sizzles. We turn the stick every few minutes so the venison will be equally scorched all over. We refill canteens, wash off blood and guts from our arms and clothes, and then force ourselves to eat the burnt barking deer. It's tough and tastes lousy, but it's better than starving, and at least it isn't monkey.

The barking deer meat gets us through the next two days, until it, too, goes bad and we have to throw it away or risk another bout of food poisoning. Well into the second day, our narrow path through jungle opens abruptly onto a wider trail. It's dusk, but Phuong insists we continue. Tall trees, hardwoods and palms, arch overhead, and Jurassic-size ferns line the way. Trees are bent over deliberately in places, sometimes dozens of them, tied from upper branches to boulders. Phuong says it's done to hide the Trail from the Americans' spotter planes, which fly low over the canopy and call in the fighter-bombers or Phantom jets to attack any NVA convoys they find.

We haven't walked far, dusk giving way to the fullness of night, when we come up on a woman dressed all in white. I jump, startled, afraid for a second that we've stumbled on a real ghost, standing there alone in the spooky darkness. Phuong speaks to her briefly, then we continue.

"Who was that?" I ask. "What's she doing here?"

"There will be others," Phuong says. "To help the drivers."

We round a curve and there's another woman, also in white. Phuong speaks to her, too.

"A convoy will be coming," she says to me after we leave the second woman. "Everywhere there's a turn in the trail, a bridge crossing, any critical location, there will be a bo doi—a trail soldier—to serve as a human road marker. Most of them are women. They wear white so the drivers can see them more easily since the trucks travel at night without their headlights on. We should be close now to the supply station where the bo doi live while they build and repair roads and pathways and escort convoys through this section of the Trail."

Though dead tired, we keep going through much of the night, passing dozens more trail soldiers in their white clothing. After a while, Phuong just speaks to them in passing, even though she says several beg her to stop and keep them company. "They'll probably be standing here all night, and the convoy may not come," Phuong says. "Or it may appear any minute." We have to be vigilant for the sounds of laboring truck engines, she adds. The last thing we want is to let our guard down and get run over, especially after all we've been through to get this far.

I stay to the side of the trail, in case I need to dive out of the way of the invisible oncoming traffic.

What shows up finally isn't a convoy of transport vehicles, though—at least not the mechanized kind. It's hundreds of bo doi pushing bicycles, each carrying an enormous load—massive saddlebags, boards across the seats with bails and boxes strapped on, bulging sacks balanced on handlebars, hundreds of pounds of food, medical supplies, ammunition, boots and uniforms, rain gear, helmets, and more. There are old men, boys, women, sometimes two to a bike, one on each side, but mostly just a single bo doi struggling to keep his or her bike and load upright and moving forward. They grunt to Phuong and their eyes widen when they see me, but no one stops. There's no conversation beyond the occasional Vietnamese hello.

It's a good half hour of them streaming past, the strangest parade I've ever witnessed. At the tail end a man does pause to speak. Phuong translates for me after he leaves—that they have to hurry, because when the trucks catch up to them there will likely be no place to pull over to let them pass—not for several miles. But the supply station is close. We'll reach there in only a few hours if we keep going tonight.

So we keep going, listening hard for trucks, for spotter planes, for more squeaky bicycles.

———————————————————

I'm asleep on my feet when we finally stumble into the supply base. More accurately, when heavily armed NVA soldiers emerge from the brush and grab us, pulling me one way and Phuong another. "Go with them," she says. "I'm sorry, but you'll have to be locked up with the other prisoners. I will find you tomorrow."

And just like that, I'm dragged off into the dark, down a path in the opposite direction of wherever Phuong goes. The path opens onto a small, treeless area, but I can't see much besides the shapes of things: other guards; a big, open cage; men lying on the ground in the cage, asleep or dead. The soldiers hand me over to young guards. The guards unlock the cage and throw me inside. I keep my distance from the bodies, but I can see that they are six Americans in ripped, tattered fatigues. None of them stir.

I find a patch of ground near the side of the cage, which is thick bamboo lashed together, topped with what appears to be razor wire. There's no roof, just a trembling night full of stars. I'm too exhausted to be afraid, or curious, or anything. I lie on my side, tuck my arm under my head, and sleep.

———————————————————

The Americans are sitting around me in a semicircle when I wake up in the morning. I struggle to sit up as well. One of them helps me. Another hands me a cup fashioned from a piece of bamboo. "Here," he says. "We saved you some water."

"Thank you," I say before tilting it back and drinking—two swallows, barely enough to wet my lips and tongue and throat.

A third GI holds out a handful of sticky rice. "Your portion," he rasps. He has a bloody rag tied around his neck.

I tuck the rice in my cheek and slowly chew a few grains at a time until they dissolve.

"I'm guessing they dumped you in our little luxury accommodations last night," the first GI says.

I nod. He introduces himself as Greg. He wears a torn dark olive T-shirt and what's left of his jungle trousers. He doesn't have on any boots or socks. None of them do. Greg's wide face is bruised and swollen. He's white. The two who gave me water and food are black. Greg introduces them, too. Darryl is the guy with the raspy voice and the bloody rag around his throat; Antwan wears a full set of tiger-stripe fatigues.

The other three guys are white. They, too, are in varying stages of dress. One can't seem to use his hands, which sit useless in his lap. Maybe he can't lift his arms, either. His buddy feeds him small nibbles of sticky rice.

"Did a girl come by looking for me this morning?" I ask, look-ing outside the cage for Phuong. I see tents, a couple of huts, stick lean-tos, but mostly trees and brush—and a few guards in over-size NVA uniforms. The guards aren't much older than kids.

Antwan snorts. "What, you lose your date last night? Got turned around on your way home and ended up here?"

I explain who Phuong is and how we got here, but that just invites more questions—and more wisecracks.

"Let me get this straight," Greg says. "You and her were alone after your other guards got obliterated, and she even passed out from bad monkey, and you didn't try to escape?"

"Man, I would have taken her AK and unloaded a round on her," says a big guy named Lloyd, the only one with a regulation army haircut. "*Then* I would have got my butt out of there."

"I didn't know where I was," I protest, annoyed that I'm hav-ing to defend myself with these guys, these fellow Americans. "I didn't know where to go or anything."

The GI with the useless hands—his name is Kyle—tells them to leave me alone already. "He's just a kid," he says. "Wouldn't none of you do any different if you didn't know any better. And it ain't like we didn't all get captured, too. And none of us run away."

Greg shrugs. "Would have if there'd been the opportunity."

They want to know how I managed to get myself captured in

the first place, and what in the world a kid like me is doing in Vietnam anyway. I tell them about Mom and Dad, and about Hanh, and the MPs, and all the rest. Greg says he might have heard of Frank Sorenson. "He's, like, one of the architects. That's what they call them. The Architects."

"The architects of what?" I ask, though I already know what he's going to say: the same thing Phuong told me about Dad.

"Stopping all the traffic coming down the Ho Chi Minh Trail," Kyle says. "Or trying to. Mostly not. Your daddy's probably one of those guys back in the embassy—they figure out what's going to work, bomb everything that moves, drown the place with Agent Orange, napalm, all that good stuff, then they send teams like us to finish up the job, see if anybody's still alive out here. Doesn't ever seem to make a difference. These North Viets, they're like cockroaches. You can't kill 'em. Doesn't matter what you do. They just keep coming, keep sending down their supplies, their weapons, their soldiers. So yeah, your daddy, pretty sure he's one of the ones behind all that. The Architects."

They ask me more questions about my getting captured and what happened after. I tell them about the underground hospital and the tunnel complex where I was tied up for three days. They say they've heard the North Viets have places like that. "They're gophers, those guys," says Greg. "Tunnels, caves, bunkers, all that underground business. Man, I'd get claustrophobia living that way. Plus you never know what kinds of creatures are down there, crawl in your food, in your bed, in your ear."

When I mention TJ and what happened to him, they say he was smart to try to escape. "Would have been a lot worse for him if he hadn't," Kyle says. "Even if it got him killed. There's worse things than getting killed, I know that for a fact."

"Must have been a spook," Darryl rasps. "I'm betting so."

"What's a spook?" I ask.

He laughs. Adjusts the bloody rag around his throat. "CIA. Probably same as your daddy."

"I don't think so," I say. "My dad's, like, the Special Attaché to something at the embassy."

They all shrug and say okay, like whatever I want to think is fine with them.

There's silence for a while after that. Then I ask how they got captured. At first they just look at one another. A couple of them shake their heads. Kyle studies his damaged hands, then speaks. "It was supposed to be a commando raid, an ambush we were setting up. We're all Army Rangers. It's sort of what we special-ize in. We got some intel, chopper dropped us at the landing site, only there they were, the North Viets, waiting for us like they knew all along we were coming."

"Like they'd got a dinner invitation, time and place and every-thing," Antwan adds.

The one guy who hasn't said anything—the other Rangers just call him J—has been sitting against the bamboo, practically catatonic. He has a red scar down the side of his face, from his temple to his jaw. J rouses himself, sits forward, and whispers, "There were a dozen of us to start out. Two six-man teams. But we're all that's left. And my bet—once they get around to finishing up their interrogations, beating out of us anything they think they can use, they aren't going to keep us alive much longer, either."

February 21

Phuong comes to the bamboo cage that afternoon with three older men, two who look like officers and a smaller man with round, rimless glasses and thinning hair, who looks like an accountant or something. They talk for a while, looking at me the whole time. Phuong is holding food but stands quietly with it and listens to the conversation, nodding when they address her but otherwise staying out of it. The accountant doesn't say much, either. He has one of those tongues that's always darting out and then back in, a nervous tic.

"Looks like they got some plans cooked up for you," Darryl rasps. There's no shade—the cage is set in the center of a small clearing—so we're sweltering under the brutal sun. The three officers—or the two officers and the accountant—leave. Phuong approaches the cage and hands me my straw hat through the bamboo, and the food in a small wooden bowl—not just sticky rice, but dried peppers, and some kind of meat.

"Tomorrow we leave to continue the journey north," she says, speaking our usual French. "You'll need to eat more for strength."

She glances at the other Americans. I put on the hat, grateful to be able to shield my face, which is blistered and raw. The food I hold on to, knowing I should share it with the others since they shared theirs with me.

"Just us?" I ask.

She shakes her head. "There will be replacements for Vu and Trang," she says. "One is a young woman, Le Phu, and her friend Khiem. They're from the same village. They've been assigned to accompany us to the next supply station, in Laos." She curls her hands around the bamboo bars, examining the places they're lashed together. She glances again at the GIs sprawled on the ground behind me. "Are you well here?" she asks.

"Yes," I say. "The ground's soft. Good for sleeping."

She smiles. "I would think you'd be used to it by now."

I smile, too, but it isn't lost on me how strange this is. The Army Rangers say I should have killed Phuong when I had the chance. They're convinced that they're going to be killed soon themselves. And yet here is Phuong, bringing me a hat and extra food, checking on me, making small talk as if it's all just a lot of polite nothing.

After she leaves I try to share the food, which would amount to a single mouthful for each of the seven of us in the bamboo cage, but our guards bang on the bars and shout orders that nobody understands. They aim their AKs and take off the safeties. Greg gets the message.

"We can't eat," he tells the others. "It's just for him."

"What?" I say. "No. I'll share it. You shared with me this morning. Really, it's okay. Here."

I offer them the bowl, but they scoot away. The guards yell louder. Nobody takes the food. I feel terrible. My stomach growls. Greg tells me to go ahead already—*Eat!*—so at least they don't have to see it or smell it. So I do, averting my gaze from their gaunt faces. I look up just once, and they're glaring. They can't help it, and I can't blame them.

I finish, lick the bowl, and hand it out to the guards. One of them snatches it from me. The other pulls down his pants and urinates through the bars, the pee splashing off the hard ground toward the Americans. Nobody bothers to move. I feel guilty for eating the food, and doing it right in front of them. But, I hate to admit, a part of me is grateful that I didn't have to share. It isn't even a matter of being grateful. It's something deeper than that. Like I'm an animal, and it's instinct, and all that matters is surviving.

Later, after the Rangers forgive me—or at least after I'm able to convince myself that they forgive me—I rejoin their ranks. They want to know what Phuong was saying, and why we were speaking French. I tell them.

"So you're out of here tomorrow?" Antwan confirms. "But now you've got three of them to guard you. You better hope there's more land mines out there for them to step on, because I don't know how you're gonna survive getting up into Laos, never mind once you're there. You have to travel over the Annamite Mountains most of the way, all steep climbs and nasty jungle that'll make what you've been through look like a city park."

"Yeah, you be careful," Greg adds. "We've been dropping what you call bouncing land mines all up and down the trail. Bump into one of them yourself and you'll wish you were dead. And that wouldn't be the worst way to get killed, either."

I ask what they know about the Hanoi Hilton, which is where I'm sure Phuong is taking me, though she still hasn't said it. But what will happen to me there, assuming I make it that far? They look at one another, at first not wanting to say. Greg breaks the silence. "He has a right to know. No sense pretending." I end up wishing I hadn't asked, as they tell me about prisoners spending months in solitary confinement until their minds snap; meat hooks on the ceiling and men tied up, their arms behind their backs, hanging from their wrists until their shoulders pop out of the socket; "hell cuffs" on prisoners' wrists that cut off circulation and cause so much nerve damage that they can no longer use their hands; men forced to kneel for hours with their arms spread like frozen wings, beaten unconscious if they move.

When they see the terror on my face, a couple of the Rangers jump in to say they're sure it will be different for me since I'm just a kid and all. I want to believe them, but I can tell by their stammering voices that they're just trying to make me feel better.

Later that day, Kyle says I should memorize all the commandos' names, so if I get back to the American side—*when* I get back, he corrects himself—I can let the world know where they were last seen and what happened to them.

"So they can come looking for us," Darryl rasps. "Last known whereabouts."

"Yeah," Antwan chimes in. "So they can at least try to find our bodies. Bury us back home. 'Cause I'd sure hate to spend all the rest of eternity stuck in Vietnam."

"Cambodia," Darryl corrects him.

Antwan lets out a dry laugh. "Wherever. Long as I'm not here."

"But you'd be dead," Greg interjects. "Why would you care?"

"You think just because you're not living and breathing, nothing matters anymore?" Antwan responds. "Man, I feel sorry for you then." He turns back to me. "You just make sure they find me and bury me back home." The way he says it, I know if he was joking around before, if all of them were, that he's not joking now.

It starts raining just after sundown. "Never expected this," Lloyd, the big guy, says, turning his face to the sky and sticking out his tongue. It's light at first, then quickly turns into a downpour. Guys cup their hands to collect it and drink. Pull their shirts off to soak up water, then squeeze it into their mouths. Fill and drink and fill and drink and fill and drink from the one bamboo cup they all share.

"Been a drought for months," Lloyd adds. "I'm betting they seeded the clouds again. And this time it worked."

Kyle, who depends on the others to collect water for him, explains that the Americans have exploded thousands of containers of silver iodide into the sky over the Ho Chi Minh Trail, hoping the rainmaking will work, first, and second, that it will turn the Trail into an impassable mud pit so no bicycles or trucks or foot traffic can make it down with weapons and supplies from the North, or if they do, that they'll be slowed down enough to essentially still choke off the supply route.

So far it hasn't worked. "And I bet there's been hundreds of missions dumping that stuff, too," Kyle adds. "But maybe tonight will be the start. Maybe it'll rain for forty days and forty nights like in the Bible, and they'll be screwed. No more reinforcements for their attack on Saigon and whatnot."

"And maybe your little girlfriend won't be able to take you away tomorrow," Greg says. "That trail turns all good and gooey, and you're either stuck here or stuck out there in it."

The rain stops after an hour, though. Not enough to affect conditions on the Trail, but enough to mean we'll spend the night wet and cold and lying in mud.

———————————

Kyle elbows me awake in the middle of the night. It doesn't take much, since I can't exactly call what I'm doing sleeping. There's a buzzing in my brain, like static on a radio or the test pattern on the TV after the station goes off the air, and I can't shake it, and I can't get comfortable enough or warm enough to do more than doze a few minutes off and on.

"Need your help," he says. "I gotta go and can't use these hands."

"Go where?" I ask, confused. The buzzing recedes when he speaks, but I still can't make sense of what he's saying.

"To the bathroom," he says. "Have to take a leak. It's embarrassing enough as it is. Don't make me have to say it again."

I peel myself off the ground and shuffle with him away from the others, who are still out cold. I've never done anything like this before, but I've never done a lot of things I can now check off my bucket list, if that's what it is. Maybe a reverse bucket list. All the things in life you never, ever, ever want to do or see or hear, but you end up doing or seeing or hearing them anyway.

I help Kyle pull his pants down, and when he finishes going I help him pull them back up. Some gets on him, but he doesn't seem to notice, or care.

"What happened to your hands, anyway?" I ask.

He lifts them halfway to his face, I guess so he can see them better in the dark. I don't know why. He can't lift them any higher because of his injured shoulders.

"You know there's twenty-seven bones in the human hand?" he says. "I didn't know that before. Antwan, he's our medic, he's the one who told me."

Kyle is quiet for a minute, then continues. "One of those guards got it in his head that he could just come in our cage and have himself a good time with a club he'd made. He took, I guess you'd call it, a disliking to a guy named Dennis. Maybe that guard just didn't like the way Dennis was looking at him. He hurt Dennis bad before I stepped in and grabbed the guard's club away from him. But that just got a bunch more of them involved, as you might expect. The guard got his club back, and while his buddies held me down he proceeded to break every one of those twenty-seven bones in both of my hands."

I don't know what to say. I feel nauseous.

Kyle doesn't wait for me to ask what happened to Dennis. He just goes ahead and tells me. "Dennis died anyway. So you might say stupid me, got my hands broken to pieces, and all for nothing."

February 22

The Phuong who comes for me in the morning is different than the Phuong from yesterday. She doesn't speak except in short bursts of angry French to order me to stand, to exit the cage, to not look back as we march away with the two new soldiers, both young like her—the girl, Le Phu, and the boy, Khiem. She orders me to keep my gaze down at my feet until we leave the camp—not that I've seen much except that handful of tents and lean-tos, and the cage.

I shake hands with all the Rangers before I leave—except for Kyle, who can only nod—my heart heavy with the knowledge that I'm probably the last American they'll ever see.

Minutes after Phuong, Le Phu, Khiem, and I reach the widened trail, a convoy of heavily loaded trucks groans up on us. We press our backs into a wall of bamboo, unable to get any farther away as the tires pass, inches from our feet. An arm reaches out of the last truck and an open palm slaps me so hard I end up sprawled facedown in the road. If there'd been another truck, I would have been crushed beneath it.

Le Phu and Khiem jerk me to my feet, the same as Vu and Trang did dozens of times when they were alive. The side of my face swells from the blow, and my eyes tear up so much that everything is blurry. I blame Phuong for not protecting or warning me. For putting me in harm's way. For not being my friend. As much of a friend as anybody could be, holding somebody prisoner with an AK-47.

Another convoy of trucks forces us into a thicket of tiger-tongue vines that rip at our clothes and tear lesions into exposed flesh. My cheek—the one that isn't swollen—now bleeds from a long cut. The convoy trucks are packed with soldiers, most of them as young as the child guards who stood watch over us in the cage. They look hungry and scared. Nobody slaps me, but a couple of them spit at me as their transport vehicles lumber by.

More groaning bicycles follow. And more bo doi on foot, bent double with strange pouches on their backs—enormous bladders that reek of gasoline. I ask Phuong what they're carrying, and she says, "Las essence." The fumes must make the carriers woozy the whole time they carry their load, hundreds of miles—never mind the weight and the awkwardness. Just as I'm thinking that, one of them staggers, and then pitches into the tiger-tongue vines.

Phuong and I help him up. We start to remove his load, a complicated harness that keeps it strapped tightly onto his back, but other trail soldiers seize him from us and drag him back into their zombie formation. They all look like the living dead when I see their faces up close. But they aren't about to stop, no matter what.

The day gets even stranger that afternoon when we encounter a parade of elephants, dozens of them, with enormous loads piled tree-high on their backs, and even more supplies on sleds that they drag behind them. Their handlers sit on the elephants' necks with iron bars they ram into holes drilled into the elephants' skulls—or that's what it looks like from ground level—I guess to control them. I shudder watching it. And I keep as far off the trail as I can get until they pass.

I ask Phuong why they're traveling during the day. "I thought the night was better, so they won't risk being seen," I say, hoping she'll speak to me. Maybe an impersonal question like that will get her to answer. Other than the occasional order and brief conversations in Vietnamese with the two new guards, it's been a quiet day, interrupted by the convoys, but that's about all.

"It's the rush to get reinforcements and weapons and more ammunition to the fight in the South," she says. "At the supply base they told me our people are still holding out against the

Americans and ARVN in Cholon. You probably don't want to hear this."

She glances at Le Phu and Khiem, as if worried they'll understand her French, as if she's said too much.

"Do they speak French?" I ask. "Is it a problem for you to talk to me now?"

Phuong shakes her head, but then contradicts herself. "Perhaps. Yes. French is considered the language of oppression, the language of the bourgeoisie, and anyone who speaks it is viewed with suspicion. They know it's necessary for me to communicate with you, but I shouldn't say too much."

Sure enough, Le Phu and Khiem are just then staring at us, frowning. They wear matching black uniforms and helmets and olive rucksacks and red scarves and green rice belts. Le Phu is shorter and has a soft face—not that that means anything. Khiem, harder and leaner, has a faint mustache and a constant scowl—except when he's looking at Le Phu.

Phuong is probably their same age, but she seems older. And she's the one in charge. I don't know why she doesn't just tell them to mind their own business. But I don't say any of that. Just the little bit of conversation we manage to have is enough to make me feel better about her.

We march on, keeping an eye out for more trucks, more fuel carriers, more bicycles, more elephants. The trail is a busy highway all that day, and the next. We split off a few times to alternate routes, but those are packed, too, all the traffic heading south. Too narrow for trucks, but room enough for bicycles, and for long lines of exhausted bo doi shuffling in sandals under cripplingly heavy loads.

Fatigue clouds my brain. We have a decent supply of rice now, and some peppers to throw in for flavor, and plenty of water as we transition through more rolling foothills to what I guess are the Annamite Mountains the GIs told me about. But my thinking becomes dulled again as fatigue sets in from the hard, forced march. Like it's all my mind and my senses can handle to just take in whatever is going on immediately in front of me. Walking. Getting out of the way. Wiping off blood from thorn scratches. Mosquitoes biting me. Slapping at them, waving them away, or watching dumbly as they draw out so much of my blood that they swell to twice their size, three times their size. Crushing them under my thumb and seeing all that blood smear. Tasting it. Spitting it out.

Both of the two nights I find myself covered with leeches after sleeping on the ground—too far gone to feel them as they attach themselves, hardly minding the pain as Phuong presses a burning stick to them to make them let go, or if they don't, just ripping them off, leaving even larger blood smears all over my arms and legs and torso and clothes.

On one of the trails, the roughest, the least developed, we come across another elephant convoy, though it isn't moving. The reason is immediately apparent: The lead elephant is stuck in a mud hole. It has slung off its load, rice and ammunition boxes everywhere, bo doi scrambling to retrieve it all before it disappears into the mud, which has the consistency and power of quicksand. The elephant thrashes around, but only manages to sink deeper. Up to its knees when we first walk onto the scene, to its belly just minutes later. Soldiers with guns are in heated discussion. One points his AK-47 at the elephant and releases the safety, ready to shoot until Phuong yells at him and he lowers his weapon. I watch the whole thing unfold as if from a distance. A part of me doesn't want them to kill the elephant. That little kid who used to go to the Bronx Zoo with his mom all the time. Another part of me doesn't care what they do. That part is happy to sit down and lean back against a tree and observe. Not my war. Not my elephant. Not my problem.

February 24

An hour later, we're still there with the elephant. Trees are cut down, ropes are pulled out, logs are rolled into the mud pit. One brave soldier leaps onto the elephant to cut loose the sled. The elephant continues to struggle, but at least he doesn't seem to be sinking any deeper. Maybe he's reached whatever hard bottom is under all that goo. The bo doi who wade in for the supplies have to be dragged out by their comrades. Phuong, Le Phu, and Khiem help. I don't move until Phuong orders me to get up and help, too.

Two soldiers beat the elephant with bamboo staffs to urge him forward, though I can't imagine the elephant feels it much. Maybe the way a human feels a gnat. Others loop ropes over the elephant's head and around his front legs. They shove more logs into the muck. The elephant shakes, swings his trunk wildly, and makes what sounds like an anguished roar, though it could just be normal elephant noise. There's more thrashing. Mud splatters everywhere, covering everybody.

The elephant surges forward. He finds one of the submerged logs to step on, then another, but then he stops, exhausted. More trees are cut down. More logs thrown in. The beatings from behind, the pulling from in front, all continue. People are yelling, as if they can order the elephant out, or coax it, or just convince it to save itself.

Finally, in a last lurching motion, the elephant gets his front legs on solid ground. Everyone cheers. But the job isn't finished. We redouble our efforts: beating, pulling, yelling. I'm into it now, too, shouting with everyone else. And then, with what seems to be a giant, involuntary spasm, the elephant crumples forward, his front legs buckling, his trunk and mouth sinking into the mud. His eyes widen in panic, then cloud over. There's more beating, more yelling, more pulling, but nothing comes of it.

The elephant slumps onto its side, and that's the end. The eyes stay open, but opaque. The mouth and trunk are submerged. There's no way he can breathe. I have to look away. I don't know why. It's just a stupid animal. Over the past three weeks I've seen people dead in just about every way somebody can be dead, but seeing this elephant die seems to be tearing me up worse.

Two soldiers, frustrated and enraged, open fire with their AK-47s, shooting and shooting until their ammo clips are empty. I glance back to see that it hasn't done much damage to the elephant. An ear tattered, half shot off. An eye exploded. Holes in its side. But it's still there. Still the same elephant. Only dead.

There's nothing to do after that. Except that the elephant is now blocking the way. The bo doi lower their weapons. I wonder what they'll do about it. Will they plant explosives and blow it up? Cut planks to lay over the mud hole and just keep going while the elephant decomposes, or wild animals emerge from the jungle and little by little tear it apart? Or maybe they'll get lucky and the air force will drop some incendiary bombs. They'll have to rebuild the trail, or redirect it through a different part of the forest. But at least they'll be rid of the obstruction.

I back away, climb on a rock, and look down on the strange tableau. Phuong is talking to the elephant handlers. Khiem and Le Phu squat off to the side of the trail. Le Phu seems upset. Khiem, his hand on the small of her back, looks to be consoling her.

For some reason, I start thinking about this German philosopher named Nietzsche we learned about in lit class. Nietzsche was walking down the street one day when he saw a man beating on an old, sick, nag of a horse pulling a heavy cart. The horse collapsed in the street, blocking traffic and attracting a crowd of gawkers. Nietzsche was horrified. He threw himself on the horse to stop the beating, wrapping his arms around the horse's neck and breaking down and sobbing right there in front of everybody.

He was never the same again. They took him to a mental hospital. Later on he thought he was Jesus, and Buddha, and various other deities. But mostly he just sat and stared at the walls in an asylum for the next eleven years until he died.

I'd copied down one thing Nietzsche wrote when he was still mostly sane, because I didn't quite understand it, but I sort of did: "Let us beware of saying that death is the opposite of life. The living being is only a species of the dead, and a very rare species."

Like, maybe there isn't all that much difference between the elephant and me. The doomed GIs back in the cage and me. Vu and Trang and me. TJ and me.

Before, I couldn't have cared less about the elephant. Now I want to do a Nietzsche and crawl in that mud pit and throw my arms around the poor animal and hold on to him so they won't hurt him anymore, or blow him up. And if I could just sit in a chair staring out a window and not move or say anything or think anything for the next eleven years like Nietzsche, maybe that would be okay, too.

We don't stay to find out what they do about the elephant. We press on for higher ground and less-traveled trails. The thick forest gives way to terraced rice paddies that climb the hills like enormous stair steps. Cambodian farmers work the fields with their buffalo and their children. The children stare when they see us passing. The adults don't bother to look. I suppose that's how it is with war. The civilians keep their heads down and try their best to live their normal lives, maybe try not to think about how it can all be taken from them in a quick burst of gunfire, or an errant bomb, or worse.

Phuong buys food from the farmers when she can. A handful of greens here and there. The occasional chicken. Most villagers are reluctant, and she never does anything that's threatening to them, as far as I can tell.

The more we walk—fifteen, eighteen hours, from before sunrise until after dark—the more everything and everyone I've ever known seems to recede. Some days I can't picture my mom's face or remember the sound of my dad's voice. My friends from school and the swim team are all a blur—kind of recognizable, but mostly out of focus. Even Geoff. I might as well have never met Beth at the Moby Grape concert, for all I can remember of her.

Snippets of songs play in endless loops in my head, but I can't come up with much of the lyrics. Dumb romance songs, mostly. Jefferson Airplane. The Doors. The Troggs. I wonder what month it is. Can it still be February? Has it already turned into March? I do the math as best I can and finally settle on the end of February.

The main thing that occupies my thoughts—that occupies every fiber of me—is food. I ask Phuong why she doesn't just take what she wants from the farmers we encounter. She doesn't like the question at all.

"We're not fighting the peasants," she says. "We're fighting *for* them. Whenever we can, it's our job to provide *them* with food. And medical care. And protection."

It sounds like propaganda, all communist sunshine and unicorns. But I suppose it's true, too. If the NVA steal food from the villagers, the villagers will hate them as much as they hate the Americans. Of course from what I've read and been told over and over by Dad, the Americans give the farmers and villagers food and supplies and medical care, too. At least we do when we aren't bombing their villages and cities, killing all their livestock, and burning everything to the ground.

I remember Dad one time talking about a place where that happened. "We had to destroy the village in order to save it," he said, somehow managing to keep a straight face.

February 28

We keep climbing. Steep slopes, unsteady footing. Loose rocks, erosion. Sudden drops, limestone cliffs. In and out of forest cover. Phuong nervously checking the sky whenever we're exposed. Twice we encounter long lines of bo doi with their crippling loads and have to press ourselves against stone walls, or balance on the edges of scary drops, while they pass. One of the columns—a hundred bo doi—carry pigs and piglets in baskets on their backs. The pigs have been sedated to keep them quiet and still.

I spend a couple of sleepless nights shivering, curled in a ball, unable to get warm, until Phuong convinces one of the columns to give me a blanket. She and Le Phu and Khiem have thin, quilted jackets that they pull from the bottoms of their rucksacks, and they wrap themselves in those and in their rain ponchos when we camp off the trail and sleep on the hard ground.

Even with the blanket, I'm cold at night, but at least I'm not freezing. The days are still blisteringly hot, especially on those trail sections with no tree cover.

Phuong is back to not speaking to me. I can't take offense, though, because she and the others don't talk much, either. I figure this is just the way it's going to be, trudging silently up and down the Annamites, which Phuong refers to as the Truong Son.

But then a freak storm catches us. One minute clear skies, and the next, black clouds, and then, a rain so hard it hurts. We're crossing one of those open sections, so nowhere to hide, nothing for cover, no choice but to keep going. I pull the blanket over my head. Phuong and Le Phu and Khiem put on their coats and ponchos and tilt their hats low on their faces. In minutes, the trail starts giving way to streams cutting down the side of the mountain, some of them so wide we have to jump over—and fight to keep our balance landing on the other side.

Phuong begins running, with the others right behind her. She yells something back to me, but it's in Vietnamese, and the rain is making too much noise for me to understand her no matter what language she uses. I hear something above me, look up to the higher reaches, and see what she must be yelling about—a wall of mud and rock sliding loose. I take off behind her as fast as my jellied legs can carry me, toward the tree line a hundred yards ahead. Twice I slip, but I manage to catch up to the others just in time to dive for cover.

The landslide continues to roar down the mountain behind us, ripping out trees, so Phuong urges me to get up again, this time in French. We aren't yet safe. The whole mountain could come down on us.

We keep running, stumbling, catching ourselves, crawling, lurching down the trail until it finally seems okay to stop, the four of us huddled under an outcropping of rock, rainwater washing in sheets over the edge, a full-on waterfall, and us hiding behind it, as if that might be the protection we need.

But somehow it holds, and the landslide doesn't reach us, and the thunder ends, and, after half an hour, the freak rain lets up and then quits altogether, leaving a thick mess of a trail ahead of us.

"We could have been killed," Phuong mutters to me in French, as if I need to be told. It seems like a funny thing to say. Every day of this trip, every hour since I was kidnapped, I could have been killed. In a hundred different ways. And I still might. Who knows what's waiting for me. And I'm sure Phuong could say that about her life the whole time she's been in the South, since leaving her home and family in Hanoi. Maybe it's the nature of this latest threat. You don't expect to be attacked by a mountain.

———

We return to the busy truck route, back down in the Truong Son foothills, but find it strangely quiet. No convoys, no bicycles, no bo doi staggering under their unwieldy burdens of fuel or pigs. The rain didn't reach this far, so every step we take kicks up dust.

There's more tree cover, so that's good, though a lot of the trees are barren, with that skeletal look we saw back in the ghost forest. Phuong says the Americans must have sprayed their Agent Orange here, but probably not in great quantities. Yet. The chemical smell is fainter than it was in the ghost forest, but still present, making me vaguely nauseous.

The silence isn't just from the absence of traffic, I soon realize. Just like back in the ghost forest and the devastation that was Ben Suc, there are no birds chirping. No insects buzzing around our heads. Our footfalls echo, but that's the only sound I hear, other than my own ragged breath.

"Maybe the war's over," I say to Phuong. "Maybe everybody went home already, and we're the last ones to know."

"You are so foolish," she says, but she smiles at me.

We continue for mile after quiet mile, grateful for the shade but growing thirstier from all the dust and the heat.

And then, rounding a deep curve and stepping out of the thinning forest, we find our answer. The trail opens onto a wide grassy field, bisected by the rutted tracks from a thousand trucks. And everywhere—dead in those tracks, dead everywhere in the field—are the smoldering wrecks of supply trucks, an entire convoy reduced to twisted metal and burning tires. And bodies. Charred skeletons. Severed limbs and torsos and heads. Blackened faces fixed in pain. Strange mounds of fire still flickering are all that remain of a hundred petrol carriers whose cargo must have erupted into flames. There are craters everywhere. Some empty. Some littered with more bodies, more wreckage, more smoldering remains. The stench is terrible. Le Phu vomits, then begins sobbing. Khiem hugs her. She buries her face in his shirt. Phuong steps forward to look for survivors, anyone who needs help, whoever she might save.

I follow, reluctantly, wading through the high scorched grass, around the wrecks and the burnt men and women, holding my breath through waves of acrid fumes. We see others who somehow survived the assault, wandering in shock, also looking for anyone still alive. Or not looking at all—too stunned themselves to even be aware of what's happened. A few stumble off into the forest, or sit down where they'd just been standing. Several times, not watching closely enough where I'm going, or my eyes tearing up from smoke, I step on brittle bones—a hand, a forearm, half of a rib cage, the flesh cooked entirely off—and they crack like twigs. The sound, and the realization, leaves me with a sick feeling, but I don't throw up like Le Phu. I can't be stoic, like Phuong, but after weeks of this, I steel myself and keep going.

We only find a few who are still alive, and they're just barely so. One begs for water while holding tightly to her belly over a massive wound, to keep her insides from spilling out. Phuong sends me to find a canteen. Ours are long since empty. I scour the field, careful about stepping on any more bodies, but I can't find anything. Except, finally, a medical pouch. I bring it back to Phuong.

"Maybe there's something in here," I say in French. "There's no water."

She rummages through the pouch and finds a vial and a syringe, somehow unbroken. She fills the syringe and injects the dying woman with whatever is in the vial. I guess it's morphine. The woman whispers something to Phuong. There's a suggestion of tears at the edges of her eyes. We sit with her for a long five minutes. Phuong keeps her hand on top of the woman's. They don't speak anymore. The woman doesn't ever cry. Instead she just dies.

We go on to help a few more survivors, none of them keep breathing for very long after Phuong injects them, too—until she runs out of morphine, and there isn't anything we can do for anyone else except wait with them until they quit breathing on their own. I don't know where Khiem and Le Phu are all this time. Maybe they went somewhere else in the field, to help others make the transition from this world to whatever world might be next. I want to believe there's a heaven, not just for believers, but for everybody, for these poor destroyed souls all dead or dying in this wretched, stinking field.

Late afternoon shadows creep in from the edges of the field and grow longer as the sun expires—way too late to be any kind of mercy.

Phuong speaks to the bo doi who have also been helping. They find ponchos that will have to do as makeshift litters, and we start collecting the dead and carrying them to the edge of the field, where we line them up for burial later. I'm back at the underground hospital carrying stretchers, carrying amputated limbs for burning. I'm back in the ghost forest doing the same thing. My brain shuts down to the horror of it all. Do the job, I tell myself. Do the job. You are the same as them, just a different species of the dead.

Finally, Phuong tells me to stop. "We have to go," she says. Khiem and Le Phu are standing there, too. I didn't see them approach. I don't know where they've been. "There's nothing else we can do to help these comrades."

"But what about graves for them?" I ask, thinking back to how efficiently the soldiers buried their dead in the ghost forest after the Dragon Ship massacre.

Phuong shakes her head. "There are too many. Word will have gotten out about what happened. They'll have heard the attack from very far away. Others will come in the darkness to dig the graves and to move the wreckage, so that more convoys can come this way tomorrow."

"Wait," I say. "They'll still use this road?"

"Yes." Phuong stands and picks up her pack. "It's how the war will be won."

I stop at the edge of the clearing to look back one last time, wondering if what I've been told is true—that this is my dad's doing, that he's one of the architects of all this devastation. A Frank Lloyd Wright of death.

March 3

That night when we camp, miles north of the carnage, Phuong spends a long time talking to Khiem and Le Phu, who seem traumatized by what we've seen. They keep weeping, hanging their heads, only whispering their responses when Phuong stops speaking or asks them questions. They don't eat their allotment of sticky rice and peppers. My stomach growls, seeing it sitting there in their cupped hands where Phuong ladles it out.

Finally, late, they lie back on the ground, their heads propped on the root flare of one of the tall trees with smooth bark. The tree branches reach high overhead, forming a cathedral arch above the small forest opening where we hide. A hot, dry wind rolls off the mountains from the west. I find my own tree to lean on, too hungry to sleep, too shaken by what we saw that afternoon, and what we had to do, to close my eyes.

Phuong comes over to check on me, too. She hasn't tied me up at night in weeks. I can't remember the last time she did it. Not that I feel any freer.

"Khiem and Le Phu haven't seen this before," she says.

"Seen the results of a bombing?" I ask.

"The war," she says. "It's their first time in battle. Or not in battle, but seeing what happens in battle. Or from your bombing of our people. They're from the same village in the North. Farm children."

"I'd never seen it, either, until I came here," I say. "Except on the TV news, and you can just change the channel when that comes on. Since Tet, it seems like I haven't seen anything else."

Phuong nods. "You become used to it in some ways. But in many ways, you never do."

We're quiet for a while. I thought she was going to ask me how I was doing, but now it seems as if she wants to be reassured herself—that we'll all get past this, that we won't be haunted by what we've seen, the things I assume she was saying to Khiem and Le Phu. Or maybe she just wants to hang out with someone, even an American, who's been through it before and doesn't need to be consoled like Khiem and Le Phu.

"What did you mean when you said this is how the war will be won?" I ask.

There's a rustling in the dark, some small night creature moving through brush. The beat of invisible wings darts past. I wonder if they're bats.

"The Vietnamese people have been fighting for independence since before I was born," Phuong says. "Even my parents saw their training, their studies in Paris, as part of the struggle. Ho Chi Minh also studied in Paris. He lived there for many years, to get to know the enemy, and to learn how to defeat them. First we fought against the French. In the Second World War, we fought against the Japanese, with the promise that Vietnam would be liberated when the war was won. But that was a lie. The Japanese were defeated, but the French returned, saying Vietnam still belonged to them. They controlled the South, but the North belonged to Ho and the Viet Minh, the party of liberation. In Hanoi, we celebrated our independence, but how do you accept a divided country? So we fought the French and defeated them at Dien Bien Phu. Once again, in the peace talks, there was the promise of elections to reunite the country. But the promise was broken. Corrupt politicians and corrupt military in the South refused to give up their control, their power. The elections never happened. We were lied to yet again. So we began the war against the South. We would have been victorious yet again, but then came the Americans."

I'd been thinking the war between North and South Vietnam was like our Civil War—the North fighting to keep their country united, the South wanting to secede. The way Phuong is talking about it now makes it also sound like the Revolutionary War, with Ho Chi Minh as their George Washington, fighting the tyranny of a foreign colonial power. For us it was the British; for them it was the French. And now, it's us.

I can tell Phuong believes every word of what she says—not just in a schoolgirl kind of way, but in her heart. She's as much a patriot for North Vietnam as my dad is for America—or the America that he's convinced has to save the world from communism, wherever it might be taking root, like in Vietnam. I've heard much of what Phuong's been saying from Geoff, of course, but I used to just figure he was repeating stuff he'd heard from his parents, the same way I used to repeat the arguments for the war I heard from my dad.

"So you see, we will never quit," Phuong continues. "We will never surrender. No matter how many of our comrades perish. No matter how many of your bombers murder our convoys of bo doi. If we have to sacrifice ten of our people for every one American life or ARVN life, that's what we are prepared to do. We sacrifice for the greater good. This must always be true of a people fighting for their own liberation."

"But you execute people," I said. "Your own people, or at least in South Vietnam. Right? The night I was kidnapped, they were going door to door. Killing Vietnamese . . ."

"Killing corrupt politicians and military leaders," Phuong says, sounding exasperated.

"Dragging people out of their beds," I say. "Probably killing them in front of their families. Murdering them. They murdered the American military police I was with."

Phuong scowls. "Don't tell me about murders," she snaps. "Did I not tell you about all the bodies of my comrades who drowned, who were shot and dumped, left to swell and rot in the Saigon River?"

"So it's war," I say. "That's it? That's the explanation for everything? The justification for whatever happens on either side, no matter how terrible?"

I know the answer even as I throw out the question. Khiem and Le Phu are sitting up now, listening to us argue in French. They pick up their weapons, as if they think they might have to protect Phuong. Or maybe they just want to get some American blood on their hands so they'll be fully initiated into the fight. They spent the afternoon hauling dead bodies out of a bombed-out field. Now's their big chance to add to the kill total.

"Yes," Phuong says quietly. "War is the explanation and it is the justification for all that happens. Terrible things will occur. People will be sacrificed. No one is innocent. No one can be free of the violence of war until the last shot is fired. And the last shot will be fired by our side. And the Americans will give up and return home. And the corruption in the South will end. And the reunification of our country will be complete. And then, and only then, there will be no more war."

"But what about communism?" I say. "You want to be like the Soviets and the Red Chinese? Like, oppressing your own people? No freedom to believe what you want to believe, or say what you want to say, or own your own business, or travel where you want, or anything?" I know I sound just like my dad, saying these things. I've heard him going on about the evils of communism a hundred times. Now I'm the broken record.

Phuong shakes her head. "You say this as if the Vietnamese people had these freedoms before, under the French. Or as if they have these freedoms now in the South, under the puppet government of the Americans. If communism gives us liberation and reunification, then of course I'm for communism. If the Soviets and the Chinese provide us with the weapons we need to fight the Americans and the ARVN, then yes to communism again. And if Ho says this is the way to bring us together as true Vietnamese people and country, then yes a third time."

I don't know what to say to all that. Probably I need to go back to my civics class and pay more attention to what we're supposed to be learning about the different forms of government, and about democracy versus communism, and all that stuff.

"It's still not right," I mumble. I smell of burning fuel and burning bodies. We all do. The whole forest does. The whole world. "All this death."

"Of course it's not right," Phuong says, which surprises me. "Parfois, il n'y a pas d'autre moyen." *Only sometimes there is no other way.*

I shut up after that. Phuong sighs and moves to softer ground. Le Phu and Khiem put down their weapons. Maybe they sleep. I do, eventually. More bats whisper past. Or maybe I dream them. Maybe it's all just a dream.

March 4

The next morning, Phuong leads us away from the wide trail. She says it's best that we climb to higher paths again through the Truong Son mountains, shift to other routes in the network of narrow paths and hidden roads that make up the Reunification Trail. It's all such a maze, I have no idea how Phuong knows her way around. She hesitates at crossroads, forks in the trail, dead ends where we have to backtrack, but we don't stop. And when we encounter others—all of them going south—there are animated conversations, pointing, gesturing, questioning glances my way, weapons raised by Khiem and Le Phu and aimed at me, for show, or that's what I tell myself, though my jaw tightens every time. I squeeze my eyes closed. I hold my breath.

Until someone hits me across the shoulders with a bamboo staff and grabs my arm jerking me forward. Then I'm their prisoner again. No longer just one of four following rolling hills, wading through swarms of black flies, skirting more landslides

198

down orange-faced cliffs, fording shallow streams. We cross grassy plains, interrupted by weathered trees that could pass as abstract sculptures you'd see in a park or at the Met in New York. Strange rock formations like something thrown there from the eruption of a distant volcano.

There are people who live in these hills, and we pass them, too. More farmers in buffalo carts, more terraced rice paddies climbing the sides of treeless hills. There seem to be dozens of different communities tucked into valleys or on the sides of these foothills. They stare as we pass. Sometimes they speak, sometimes they wave. Sometimes their children look fearful and start crying. Sometimes their children sit motionless on the backs of their water buffalo and don't pay us any mind.

We come across an abandoned coffee plantation. All the furniture has long since been stripped clean, so we sleep on the wood floor, or what's left of it. Khiem breaks up boards for a small indoor fire. Phuong and Le Phu leave for an hour and come back with food. Spicy buffalo to go with our daily serving of sticky rice and peppers. They don't say where they got it, but I assume they found a village.

Finally, after a week of hard travel, we enter another hidden supply base—so well camouflaged that guards blend into the brush, and even when I hear them move I can't make out their faces or their forms until they step forward menacingly. Phuong quickly shows them her papers and explains who we are and why we're there.

Inside the compound, there are logs shoring up the entrance to underground bunkers, and tall trees bent over to form dense canopy, held there with cables tied to heavy stones. Spotter planes would have to fly so low to see what's there that anyone with an AK-47 could easily take them out. And everyone there has an AK-47. There are also antiaircraft weapons, dozens of trucks, repair bays, a huge underground cache of rice, and another filled with weapons and ammunition. For some reason, they let me see all of this as we're led through the camp, which goes on for half a mile, following a brown-water stream. Phuong disappears into another bunker at some point, leaving us next to a pen with a herd of wild boar banging around inside, waiting for slaughter. Boy-faced soldiers stand guard over a sea of chickens. Small fires burn. There's even running water of a sort—a sluice made from split bamboo lashed together and streaming down from the creek, emptying into barrels. We're offered food, and the strips of boar meat are a definite improvement over buffalo. Back home I thought of myself as a casual vegetarian. Cheese pizza, french fries, and sugar cereal made up 90 percent of my diet. Vietnam has turned me into a desperate carnivore.

We spend the night at the supply base—on the ground, as usual—with hundreds of bo doi. There are no tents, no buildings except the bunkers, no cover except the trees. I keep expecting to be thrown into another cage, to meet other prisoners, to see more brutality. But here, nobody seems to care. I'm a passing curiosity to some of the bo doi, but that's all. I keep close to Phuong when she returns—anxious that I'm missing something, that things might go south any second.

I barely sleep. All night long, vague figures come and go through the compound. The small fires from earlier are extinguished. There's no light, except what little filters through the canopy from the moon and the stars. Deep in the night, from out of nowhere, I'm hit by a frantic attack of loneliness and homesickness and worry about Mom and Dad—a certainty that they are dead, and that I'm all alone in the world. I tell myself that Dad must be alive, though, or why else would they be going to all this trouble with me, unless they think they can use me for a prisoner exchange, because of who he is. And Dad would never let anything happen to Mom, no matter how many NVA attacked the embassy in Saigon on Tet.

It's little reassurance and longer into the night, I'm still anxious and think about waking Phuong up, asking her to talk to me—about anything, about nothing. Just for the company. Just for a familiar voice.

I know how crazy and ironic it is, that the only closeness I feel in this dark hour is with the person taking me farther and farther away from everything and everyone I've ever known.

I don't know where we are, what country we're in. I think maybe we're still in Cambodia, but we could just as well have crossed back into Vietnam, or into Laos. Not that it matters. Not that I think I'll be rescued from the Trail through some movie miracle.

Has it only been a couple of weeks since the monkey stew, and the food poisoning, and holding on to Phuong, pressing my body against hers to warm her as she shivered so violently, until her fever broke?

I can just make out the contours of her face where she lies near me, on her side. There's a softness that I haven't seen before. Wisps of straight black hair fall over her cheek, and I want to reach over and brush it back. It's stupid thinking about her like that—like I would a girl back home, like Beth maybe. Phuong isn't a girl. She's a soldier, doing her job, delivering me up to a prison in Hanoi where they might make a deal to let me go home again, or they might kill me.

On the trail the next day, an hour after leaving the compound, I ask Phuong once again where we're going.

"I've told you many times already," she says. "North. I can't say more than that."

"I mean the route we're taking," I say. "The direction. What country we're in now, and what country we'll be in tomorrow. The next place we'll be where there are people. The next supply base or whatever."

Phuong sighs, like I'm asking pointless questions, but she answers anyway. "We're still in Cambodia. We'll climb back higher through the Truong Son mountains into the Three Borders area, where Cambodia meets with Vietnam and Laos. We'll go to Nong Fa to rest for a few days, just inside the border with Laos, then continue on from there."

"Nong Fa?"

"Yes. It's also called the Lake in the Sky. I was there once before. It's a beautiful place, with orchids growing on the bark of pine trees all around the shore. Nong Fa was created from a volcanic crater. It's very high, and very cold, and the local people claim that anyone who swims in it will have eternal youth."

"I could probably use some of that," I say.

March 11

The next few days pass quietly—except for the sounds of our ragged breathing as we drag ourselves up steep paths, stumbling and sliding on loose rock. We're in and out of forests, sweating under thick tree canopy, wading through tangles of creepers, spiky ferns, and naked, leafless understory saplings fighting their way through openings in the green ceiling and into the light.

The trail we're on clearly isn't one of those well traveled. And definitely no trucks could ever fit here; at most the path is maybe six feet wide. Twice we wade across streams waist deep, Phuong anxious the whole time—so much so that she holds her weapon over her head with one hand and hangs on to Khiem's rucksack in front of her with the other. When her foot slips on a slick rock she screams and then is embarrassed, not looking at any of us for a good hour as we continue up the trail.

We come to a deep ravine that seems impossible to cross until we find a giant tree with boards nailed up the trunk. We climb to a branch so wide I could sleep on it, and from there we have to step out onto a narrow cable, with two more cables head high to hang on to. The cables—and our knees—shake wildly as we struggle to keep our balance the whole way across, with a river crashing forty feet below us, until we get to the other side and another giant tree, which we take turns hugging.

There's a rhythm to our days, with enough water that our canteens are never empty, enough wild boar to go with our sticky rice and peppers and keep our bellies full, or sort of full, anyway, and to give us the strength for all the climbing and fording and balancing we have to do to keep going. The jungle still crowds the sides of the trail, heavy trees growing together in an unbroken wall of green. At times it seems as if we're walking in another underground tunnel, only without the stale air and dripping rock walls.

We emerge from one of those claustrophobic sections of trail when Khiem signals for us to stop. Something small and black and furry darts out of the brush and stops in the middle of the trail. It sits on its bottom, facing us, blinking. A bear cub. Le Phu whispers to Phuong, who shrugs and takes a hard step forward to scare the cub off the path. It doesn't move. Just blinks some more, and then opens its mouth and lets out a sound that's a cross between a yawn and a growl. Like a little kid's attempt at a growl.

Khiem jumps up and down, yelling. The cub stirs, scoots backward, slaps the ground, but stays.

A flock of birds shake themselves free from the upper branches of a tree and fly off. Something crashes through the brush. I should know what it is. I saw that movie *Old Yeller*. The mama bear always shows up when her cub is in trouble. The mama bear always attacks.

This one is no exception. She emerges suddenly, rears back on her hind legs, paws raised, claws out, mouth open, fangs showing. She roars, leaps forward, and charges.

Le Phu doesn't have time to even swing her AK-47 from her shoulder before the bear is on her, knocking her to the ground and swatting at her face with an enormous paw. I see a spray of blood, hear her scream. There's an explosion of gunfire, right next to me, as Phuong and Khiem unload on the bear. She pulls herself up, swats at the bullets ripping through her fur and her flesh, reels back toward the cub, falls. The explosions continue, tearing off chunks of the bear's face, her legs, her torso. A large white triangle on the bear's chest turns crimson as blood spurts out of a dozen bullet holes. Phuong and Khiem keep firing until their clips are empty, just as the NVA soldiers did to the drowned elephant.

The bear is still alive, though just barely, trying to drag herself away, not off the trail but closer to the cub. Once there, she collapses and doesn't move again.

Le Phu is lying half-on and half-off the trail, one side of her face a bloody mess, most of the skin peeled off. Bone showing on part of her scalp. A patch of hair torn out. She might have lost an eye. Phuong and Khiem crouch beside her. Khiem holds on to her. She's writhing in pain and moaning, though her mouth isn't moving, probably because her jaw is broken.

I look back up the trail where a spreading pool of blood soaks the earth, pouring out from under the bear. The cub whimpers, though it's hidden and I can't see it. Maybe it's trapped under the mother. I wonder if I should help it get free. I wonder what we can possibly do for Le Phu. We'll have to carry her, but how? And where? We can't go back to the last supply camp. We'll never be able to cross the cable bridge. Or wade with Le Phu through the waist-deep rivers. And never mind the rivers and streams. Do any of us even have the strength to carry her up and down these mountain paths?

As terrible as it is to think such a thing, a part of me hopes she'll die right here by the trail, saving us the trouble. Not just the trouble, but the impossible task of trying to save her.

But then Le Phu struggles to lift herself. Phuong and Khiem help and hold her in a sitting position. Khiem lifts his canteen to her lips and she drinks, or tries to. Most of it dribbles out of the wounded side of her mouth where her lips are shredded. She coughs and moans. She spits out teeth and blood.

I join them, and we carefully lift Le Phu and carry her to a tree to prop her up. She tries to speak, but I don't think Phuong and Khiem can understand her. They shake their heads.

Phuong searches through her pack for her small medicine kit, which doesn't contain much. There's some sort of ointment that she tries to apply to the massive wound on Le Phu's face, but Le Phu pulls away. Phuong tries again, and a third time, but it's too painful. Le Phu begs her to stop. That's what I guess, anyway, though the sounds coming from deep in her throat may not be actual words.

In the end, Phuong wraps gauze around Le Phu's face—her jaw, her cheek, her ear, her eye socket, over the top of her head, covering the missing hair. She looks like a mummy, though with her good eye, her nose, and most of her mouth uncovered. She can still drink, sort of. And she can still breathe and she can still see out of her one good eye.

So she isn't going to die. That much is clear now, and I feel ashamed of myself for wishing it before. I don't know what to think about where my mind went in the aftermath of the bear attack. What's wrong with me that all I care about, or the first thing I care about, is how Le Phu losing half her face, and maybe her life, might affect me, might be an inconvenience? Have I always been this way, or can I blame it on the war? On being kidnapped? On all the horrors I've seen since Saigon?

I shake myself out of that reverie. Another voice in my head reminds me that Le Phu is also the enemy, just like Phuong, just like all the bo doi we've encountered on the Trail, whether they've been mean, or kind, or indifferent. She pointed her weapon at me numerous times and with one squeeze of the trigger could have killed me. Phuong said she was new to the NVA, but that only meant she hadn't shot at American soldiers—*yet*.

Phuong and Khiem pull Le Phu to her feet. I can't believe it, but she manages to stand. She sways, reaches for Khiem's arm to steady herself, then points to her AK-47 in the weeds, and to her rucksack. He helps her put them on. She sways again, but once more steadies herself on his arm, and then, without another word, they start down the path like an old married couple, her leaning on him, shuffling her feet at first, then gradually establishing an even pace, him setting the direction and leading the way.

Phuong and I try to drag the bear off the trail, but she's so heavy we can barely budge her. Just enough to uncover the trapped cub.

She presses the barrel of her AK-47 into the cub's ear and pulls the trigger. My heart's gone stone cold. I don't even flinch.

March 13

Phuong and Khiem take turns helping Le Phu walk. When I offer, she recoils as if I'm a viper. Phuong says I can just carry Le Phu's pack and rice sling. Phuong takes her weapon.

We stop frequently to rest. Blood soaks through the gauze on Le Phu's face. Phuong changes it after a few hours, when it gets so bad that it's dripping onto her shirt and leaving a blood trail behind us. Dead flesh and scabbing tear off when Phuong peels away the gauze, and Le Phu faints. I think we'll stop for the night, but when Le Phu wakes up she insists that we go on.

So we do, following a ridge trail until dusk. Phuong lets us build a small fire to heat the last of the wild boar strips, which are starting to go bad. Le Phu can't chew, can barely get any food into her mouth. Khiem chews the food for her, rice and boar, and then carefully, as gently as he can, tucks each bite into Le Phu's cheek on her good side. She sucks on it, swallows, and waits for more. She's so worn out that she doesn't bother to lift her hands to accept the food, or do it herself. Or maybe she just doesn't have the strength. Khiem continues feeding her, like a mama bird and a baby bird, until Le Phu shakes her head to make him stop.

The gauze is soaked through again, but Phuong doesn't have anything to replace it and is reluctant to pull off the old gauze anyway, for fear of the pain it will cause. There's yellow seepage in places mixed with the blood.

Le Phu sleeps, or tries to, leaning on Khiem, who sits up all night propped against a tree so he can hold her. I hear them, or hear him, whispering. Someone is crying, but I can't tell in the darkness if it's him or her. I had wondered if they were a couple. I don't wonder anymore.

In the morning, Le Phu is flush with fever, but there's nothing to do for her except press forward, Phuong and Khiem practically carrying her as she slips into delirium and keeps trying to leave the trail, pointing and grunting at things we can't see. She finally lets me help, or just isn't aware that I'm helping. Khiem won't let go of Le Phu. He stays on one side; Phuong and I take turns on the other, whoever is with her soon drenched in sweat—hers, our own.

When Le Phu's knees buckle and she slumps to the ground, we stop to rest. When she fights her way back to standing, we start again.

___

The day before there was a bear cub in the middle of the trail. Now, late that afternoon, there are suddenly children. Just like

211

the cub, they stand blinking at us. Then they plunge into the forest.

We follow, fighting our way through vines, tripping over creepers, trying to keep close to the sound of them so they'll lead us to their village. Khiem and I pick up Le Phu and carry her, as Phuong leads the way, hacking at saplings and low branches that block us, until finally the forest opens up, giving way to a dirt clearing. The kids we've been chasing are huddled behind their adults, pointing at us and talking excitedly in their language.

The grown-ups don't share their children's excitement. Two men wearing loincloths and T-shirts approach us. Phuong gestures at Le Phu's face, mimics the bear attack—fingers spread like claws, swiping at her own face. The men nod and lead us to a longhouse on log stilts across the clearing. It has a high thatched roof, with smoke rising through the thatch. Inside, it's too dark to see anything until our eyes adjust to the deep gloom. There are several women squatting around a small fire. The walls are black from smoke. Straw pallets line the floor on one side, and they have us lay Le Phu on one of them.

An old woman comes over with water in a metal container that I realize is an army helmet. American. The old woman bathes Le Phu's face and then starts taking off her clothes. Phuong pulls Khiem and me out of the longhouse, shoves us down the wobbly steps, then goes back inside to help.

Khiem and I sit on the ground outside, too tired to move. The kids keep their distance. An old man shuffles over with another army helmet filled with water, and we drink it all, nodding our thanks. A woman brings us each a whole fish that has been cooked so black that it's like eating dust. But we eat it, even the bones, which are hardly bones anymore, they're so brittle.

Khiem takes Le Phu's rucksack from me, for no real reason other than I guess he just doesn't want me to have it. He won't look at me. There's no point in trying to talk. We don't speak the same language. Several of the villagers come over, but Khiem can't make out what they're saying any better than I can. We both shrug helplessly. Khiem leans back on his post, and I lean back on mine. He closes his eyes, and I close my eyes, half to signal to the villagers that we don't want to try to communicate with them anymore, half because we're too exhausted to keep them open.

Phuong comes out after an hour to tell us Le Phu is dead. First Khiem, in Vietnamese. He buries his face in his hands and just sits there shaking. Then me, in French. "Elle est morte." But I've already figured it out. I don't know how to react, so I don't.

Phuong puts her hand on Khiem's shoulder, for a second, then goes back inside to see to the body.

All that work getting here, I think. All that work to survive. Le Phu fighting and fighting through the wound and the blood, her

213

eye destroyed, her jaw shattered, the infection, the fever. Phuong and me and Khiem carrying her. Not giving up. Never giving up. And for what?

The kids are oblivious, still running around the swept-dirt clearing, playing a game, rolling heavy balls at one another, half a dozen of them, the size of fists. The game seems to be a cross between marbles and dodgeball. I watch idly, not seeing much point to it. But they're having fun, dancing out of the way when one is rolled at them. Rolling their own at their friends.

Khiem lifts his face but doesn't move otherwise. His cheeks are wet, his eyes red. The kids sweep back and forth in front of us with their game. The grown-ups have disappeared, except for a couple of elderly men sharing a bamboo cup. They laugh, slap each other on the back. One lights a long thin pipe. They pass that back and forth, too.

Shadows grow as the afternoon fails. I don't see the point of anything. Ridiculous as it is, I start humming a new song by the Beatles, "Magical Mystery Tour." It was the last record I bought back in New York. Actually I stole it, not because I didn't have the money, but just for the stupid thrill of shoplifting. It was right before Christmas. A lifetime ago. Ten lifetimes.

I don't want to think about Le Phu lying inside the long-house. I don't know how to reach out to Khiem to comfort him, and he wouldn't let me anyway. He probably wants to kill me, because aren't I the reason Le Phu got attacked? Why wouldn't he hate me? *If only we hadn't been assigned to take this stupid American to the North, Le Phu would still be alive. But the American, he's the one who should be dead.*

It's what I would have been thinking.

I start singing the Beatles song under my breath. It isn't lost on me how ironic it is. Like I'm on some magical mystery tour of my own, only dark and deadly instead of the Beatles on a painted bus raging through the English countryside with their goofy soundtrack.

Phuong comes back out. I hear her on the steps behind us. I turn to look. She looks so sad; it breaks my heart to see her like that.

The kids squeal, still playing their game, though it's growing dark now. Phuong's expression changes. Her eyes widen, her jaw drops open, she yells. She flies past Khiem and me, racing toward the kids.

They stop to stare. One picks up his ball. Maybe he's going to give it to her.

There's a bright flash, an explosion. There's smoke. The kid is sitting on the ground, holding up his arms. What's left of his arms. His hands are gone. His arms are bloody stumps. He tries to say something. He can't speak. His friends freeze around him. One is lying on the ground ten feet away, not moving.

Phuong is knocked down by the blast. She gets up and goes to him, but it's already too late. The boy with no hands reaches for her. She takes him in her lap and strokes his hair. Khiem quietly approaches the other kids and slowly, carefully, lifts the heavy balls out of their hands.

There's so much death in this village. There's so much death everywhere.

March 14

They're cluster bombs. Or bouncing bombs. Or bomblets. Or even, sometimes, bombies. They go by different names. The commandos in the bamboo cage warned me about them, warned me to be careful, to be on the lookout, but I forgot. The bomblets are contained in larger bombs, which are designed to open before hitting the ground, releasing the bomblets. The bomblets, each with its own little parachute, land near the Trail. Or they blow far off course. There are millions of them.

Some explode when they hit the earth. Some bounce and explode at the level of a torso, or a head. Some explode when trucks run over them. Some explode when bo doi kick them accidentally. Some, buried in fields or lost in the forest, explode when buffalo step on them, or plows hit them, or branches fall on them, or night animals sniff them, or birds perch on them, or the wind blows heavy on them. Some never explode. They're duds. Some explode for no clear reason after kids discover them in the forest, and carry them to their village, and play with them for hours, rolling them on the ground like bocce balls, jumping over them, stopping when a stranger, a Vietnamese soldier, steps out of the longhouse and yells at them, in a language they don't understand, to stop.

Khiem herds the children and villagers away from the clearing and into the forest, taking the bodies of the two dead kids with them—the one who was holding the cluster bomb, the other who was hit in the forehead by shrapnel. Once everyone is safe, Khiem aims his AK-47 at the remaining bombs and fires. The explosions leave small craters in the packed earth.

Le Phu is buried. The kids are buried. One of the villagers, perhaps the mother of one of the dead children, kneels and wails and hits herself on the head over and over with a large, flat stone. Others stop her, but not before blood streams down her face.

We leave soon after. No one in the village acknowledges our departure. They aren't angry. At least they don't seem to be. Maybe they're resigned to this—to losing children to a war that they know somehow, distantly, is going on around them, but I doubt they understand. I barely understand it myself, and I've grown up with it on the news.

I can't shake the images: of the little boy right after the explosion, reaching with his bloody stumps for Phuong, mouth open but no sound coming out; of Phuong holding the dying child in her lap; of Khiem, still numb from the loss of Le Phu, collecting bombies from the other children.

And I can't shake the question that won't go away, though I already know the answer: Can my dad be the architect of *this* as well?

===

Another freak rainstorm catches us the next day on the side of a mountain, and we're exposed to everything the sky hurls down at us, as if we deserve it. We trudge through for hours, slipping on the muddy trail, climbing around places where the trail is washed away, looking for any shelter but finding none. We come to a cliff, with wooden stairs lashed together and nailed or tied to the sheer rock face, a steep climb that we have to make. Below us is a sharp drop with boulders and a river at the bottom. Above us is the promise of a return to the ridge trail, and maybe a cave where we can dry off and sit out the deluge.

The stairs wobble dangerously. With all three of us on them, they pitch in unpredictable directions. I can't believe they'll hold us, but Phuong assures me that hundreds, thousands of bo doi have made this passage with their heavy loads of supplies. "These trails will be used until the Americans discover them, and then abandoned until the Americans forget," she says. I'm supposed to take solace in this, but my legs and arms are trembling too much.

We're a third of the way up when the rain quits. We're halfway up when we hear the whine of a twin-engine plane cresting the horizon. Phuong and Khiem press their backs against the cliff, brace themselves, and unshoulder their AK-47s. An American spotter plane flies at us from the north, so close that I can see the face of the pilot, just for a second. Khiem fires a short burst, and the plane veers away but doesn't leave. It circles around and comes back at us from the south. This time an arm reaches out the passenger window—with a hand holding a pistol. Bullets ricochet off rocks a few feet above our heads, sending a spray of dust and pebbles raining down.

"I'm an American!" I yell as loud as I can. "American! American!" I pull off my straw hat and wave it at the plane. Khiem slams the butt of his weapon into my chest. I stagger, think I'm going to pitch over the side, grab the safety rope, and barely manage to hang on. Khiem raises his gun to hit me again, but Phuong stops him. At first I can't breathe. He's knocked the wind out of me. Then, when I get my breath back, I feel the ache of a deep bone bruise. It hurts to breathe. Khiem tugs me to my feet, shoves me ahead of him, and jams the barrel of his AK-47 into the small of my back to force me the rest of the way up the wooden stairs.

It takes forever, every arduous step more painful than the one before, every breath a knife to my ribs. Khiem keeps jabbing me with his weapon, barking at me in Vietnamese. Twice when I slow too much he hits me higher, at the base of my skull. I pitch forward. He grabs my shirt and jerks me upright. Phuong, in the lead, doesn't know any of this, or maybe she knows and chooses to ignore what's happening.

Khiem isn't through. When we finally crest the ridge and climb off the wooden stairs, I don't even have a chance to sit before he starts hitting me with his fist—keeping his AK trained on me the whole time. I double over from a blow to my stomach, then to my chest. He slaps me hard, twice, in my face. The third time I cover myself, but that just makes him angrier. He trips me, and when I fall he kicks me wherever he can—my legs, my back, my shoulder, my arms, the back of my head.

I curl into a fetal position, wrap my arms over my head, struggle to pull away when I see where he's kicking me next. He catches me anyway, and there's nothing I can do about it. I vomit blood. Phuong finally intervenes, yelling at him, stepping between us, pushing Khiem away.

I want to hurt him back. I want to kill him. I hate him, and hate what he's done to me, leaving me scared and helpless—and raging inside, with no way to let it out. I can't even yell at him, curse at him, anything. I pound the dirt with my fist, spit up more blood, sit up sobbing, snot running down my burning face. My jaw aches. I'll have bruises all over my arms, legs, back, face, everywhere. I'm afraid Khiem broke one of my ribs when he slammed his gun into my chest on the stairs—that's how bad it hurts to take anything more than a shallow breath.

"We can't stay here," Phuong says. "We're too exposed. The Americans might return."

She's right. There's no tree cover, no cave, no shelter of any kind. Just barren rock, a moonscape. We make for the tree line, a quarter mile away. I swear that if Khiem gets behind me again, if he stabs me one more time in the back with his weapon, I'm not going to be afraid. I'm going to fight. I seethe and wait for the moment, that deep well of anger powering my legs forward. But Khiem keeps his distance. Phuong tells him to take over the point position—the lead—so he passes ahead of me. I could jump on him from behind, grab a rock and pound his head in, seize his weapon and kill him and make my escape.

Only I'll probably get killed instead—by him hearing me make my move, or by Phuong, to protect him.

March 15

"Khiem—his heart is broken. You should know this. He was in love with Le Phu."

I can barely hear Phuong's quiet voice over the cacophony of insects that night. It's hard to sleep through the noise, reminding me that I've only occasionally heard them on the Trail. Or birds. Or night animals. We're inside a shallow cave Phuong found, just as darkness was taking hold. She let us build a small fire that was mostly smoke from green wood. We ate sticky rice. We hadn't asked the villagers for food, so there wasn't anything else.

"Why are you telling me that?" I ask, not bothering to open my eyes. My eyelids feel too heavy, too bruised. Everything about me is sore.

"So you'll understand why Khiem did what he did," she says. "It wasn't just because you shouted to the American plane."

"Whatever you say," I respond curtly. "You don't have to explain anything. It's war. We're enemies. I get it."

"Yes," she says. "And we have our orders, and we follow our orders. But . . ."

She stops.

"But what?" I ask.

"Just, I shouldn't have let Khiem hurt you like that. It wasn't right. I knew he was suffering, that he was angry and grieving. Khiem blames you for what happened to Le Phu."

I clench my jaw, though it aches. I don't want to feel sorry for Khiem. I don't want to have sympathy for Phuong, for Le Phu, for anyone. I just want to go home.

"I think he broke my rib," I say. "It hurts when I breathe. Everything hurts from where he hit me. And you let him."

"I know," she says softly. "I'm sorry for that. But you're right that this is war, and it's the only explanation for much of what happens that can't be justified, just as we talked about before. The harshness. The brutality. The indiscriminate deaths. Those kids in the village, the people. How can there ever be enough justification for their lives ending in that terrible way? How can there be justification for their lives ending at all, at their young age? When I was a kid, I played with my brothers and sisters, with my friends at school. My parents took care of us. They made sure we attended to our studies. That we burned sacrifices to our ancestors. That we took care of our grandparents. That we supported the cause of liberation.

"That was before the bombings. Before we heard so many stories of sacrifice, knew so many who went to fight but never returned, or who were wounded, or who were maimed, or who were never again right in their minds. The only way to see this and continue fighting, is to believe in the cause, that it is right and just and that we will prevail. In war, both sides must think this way. But for our side, sacrificing so much more than yours, we can't afford to question. We can only persist through all that must be endured."

Phuong grows quiet. The insects do as well, which is strange. Like somebody shushed the whole night.

"Do you want to come sit with me in the mouth of our cave?" she asks after a few minutes. "I can't sleep yet. I heard you tossing and turning. I know you haven't been able to sleep, either."

"What about Khiem?"

She laughs quietly. "You haven't heard him snoring all this time?"

We move to the opening, her in her quilted mountain jacket, me wrapped in my thin blanket, and lean against a boulder to look up at the stars.

"You know about constellations?" I ask.

"I doubt I know them in the same way you do," Phuong says.

"Same stars, though, right?" I ask. "I mean the same ones I would see back in America. Because we're both in the Northern

Hemisphere?" Not that you can ever see stars at night over New York. But there's always the Hamptons.

"Yes," she says. "I believe they're mostly the same stars. Maybe that means something."

"Yeah," I say. "Maybe."

Bats come out, darting past our faces. I can't tell if they're leaving the cave or returning to it. Or if they just happen to be in the vicinity.

"I told you where we're going," Phuong said, a bat whispering by so close that it ruffles her hair.

"To the Lake in the Sky," I say.

"Yes. To Nong Fa," she says. "What I haven't told you is where we are ordered to take you after, and why we are taking you there first."

"Are you going to tell me now?" I ask.

She takes a deep breath and lets it out slowly.

"I shouldn't tell you this. I have my orders, and those must be followed. But sometimes it's hard. I know how anxious you've been. Anyone would be."

I wait.

She continues. "You were told you can be useful to us. My superiors decided to keep you alive, as a prisoner, and for us to take you to Hanoi, where you might have some propaganda value.

And where you might be used in a prisoner exchange for some of our people because your father is CIA."

"I don't know that for sure," I say, simultaneously relieved and terrified to have her confirm what I've already known, or at least deeply suspected, all these weeks.

"It doesn't matter," she says. "They *believe* he's CIA. And so the instructions are to escort you to Hanoi. But my superiors decided there's another way you can also be useful."

"How?" I'm trying to stay calm, but my voice—and my hands—are trembling at the thought of the Hanoi Hilton and what will happen to me there.

"They have identified a man, an officer assigned to the supply station where we stayed in Cambodia, who they suspect is a spy for the Americans. You may remember seeing him."

"When you came with three men to the bamboo cage? Was it one of them? The spy?" I'm still fighting to keep from letting on how shaken I am.

"Yes," she says. "A smaller man with glasses. He was told that you are the son of Frank Sorenson, one of the CIA architects of the war on the Reunification Trail. He was also informed that our destination in Laos is Nong Fa and he was given the date we are expected to arrive."

"Okay," I say. "So?"

"No one else was told this information. If this man is a spy, we believe he'll contact the Americans to let them know where they might attempt to rescue you. And if the Americans attempt to rescue you at Nong Fa, then it will be confirmed that this man is the traitor."

"So I'm like, what, the bait?" This just keeps getting worse and worse.

"Yes," she says.

"But what will happen? I know you won't let them take me."

"No. A unit of our commandos will be there, unseen, waiting for the Americans. There will be an ambush."

"And they'll be killed," I say, crestfallen.

"Perhaps the Americans will retreat," she says, though I'm not buying it. "Maybe they'll pull back to safety and give up on the mission. It doesn't matter either way—whether they stay and fight and perish, or whether they turn and run. Because if they show up at all, we'll know about our spy, and he can be dealt with."

"What happens to me?" I ask.

"You and Khiem and I will continue to the North," she says.

"Why are you telling me all of this?" I ask.

"Because you saved me," she says. "Twice. And I haven't forgotten. You are a prisoner and have every reason to hate me. To want to kill me. And yet, you saved my life. I didn't know why. I still don't."

The silence swells between us, until she adds, "If the Americans show up, I want you to stay close to me. It will probably turn violent and keeping close to me is the only way you'll be safe. I've been ordered to stay clear of the firefight if it should happen."

"And if I run? If I try to warn them about the ambush?"

"You won't make it," she says. A pause. And then, "If you run, if you try to warn them about the ambush, I'll have to kill you myself."

March 16

The rest of the trek to Nong Fa is long and slow. Khiem spots a red-bellied squirrel in a fight for its life with a tree snake, or maybe it's the other way around. Either way, he kills both with his machete and roasts them on sticks over a small fire Phuong lets him make. He divides the meat for him and her, and acts annoyed when Phuong shares hers with me. He speaks to her sharply in Vietnamese, but she doesn't respond. I don't care, as long as he doesn't hit me again. I eat snake and squirrel for the first time and am happy to have both.

My injuries heal quickly, making me think my ribs aren't broken after all. Breathing gets easier, though the deep bone bruise in my chest is still painful to the touch. Other bruises, the ones I can see, fade to blue, then green, then yellow. I have no idea what my face looks like. My hair has grown out so long that I tie it back into a ponytail with a piece of string from Phuong—until she offers to chop it off with her knife. I figure it will be easier to have it short, so I let her.

We keep to mountain trails, crossing streams on more shaky cables, dragging ourselves up stone steps carved into limestone cliffs, scrambling over and around boulders blocking the path, sleeping in caves or under rocky overhangs. It doesn't rain again—still months until the rainy season—but it's nice to have the cover just in case.

Twice we meet columns of bo doi making their way south, bent forward under their supply loads, staggering up the trails we walk down, sometimes tumbling down the stone steps we ascend. We help bury two who die from their falls. Others who are injured just find a way to continue. Some express surprise to see an American on the Trail, but most are so fatigued, with so far still to go, that they don't bother.

Every step closer to Nong Fa fills me with dread. There will be a rescue attempt. Maybe. Or maybe it will just be a break in the trip north and nothing more. I don't know which one to hope for. I don't want anyone to be killed trying to save me; I don't want to be buried in a Hanoi prison. How could they ever let me go in a prisoner exchange? I probably know too much. I replay the conversation with Phuong over and over in my mind. A squad or a company or maybe a whole battalion of NVA commandos will be there to ambush the American rescue team. If there is any truth to one of those men being a spy back at the Cambodia supply station, I know Dad will do whatever it takes to rescue me. Maybe he'll even come to Nong Fa to save me himself.

But what if he does come? He could be killed. The rescue team could be slaughtered. And it will be my fault. I have to think of something, anything. But even if I run away right now, somehow get away from Phuong and Khiem, I have no way to warn anybody.

The only chance I have is to go to Nong Fa and look for an opportunity to somehow signal the rescuers that it's a trap. Maybe Phuong is tired of the war, tired of all the killing. Maybe she told me about the spy and the rescue and the ambush not to stop me from warning the Americans, but to make sure I do, so they can escape. So that I can get away, too.

I shake my head to clear it out, because even as I have those thoughts, I know how ridiculous they are. Stupid daydreams about playing hero, saving the day, being John Wayne. Why don't I just grab a machine gun and shoot down all the bad guys while I'm at it?

I have a distant memory of having prayed not long after I was captured, but no memory of any prayer being answered. But maybe that isn't the point of prayer. I haven't been to church enough to know, but I think maybe it's a comfort thing. I decide to try again, and start off well enough: "My God." Only the prayer doesn't progress any further. Just "My God," over and over, like a heartbeat. After a while it *is* my heartbeat. *My God, My God, My God. My God.*

Mon Dieu, Mon Dieu, Mon Dieu.

━━━━━━━━━━━━━━━━━━━━━━━━

The trail takes us to high ridges as we continue our journey, with long views of rolling mountains, rising one after another like a pod of great whales swimming through a green ocean. In the early mornings, the world is soaked in mist, which gradually settles into valleys, leaving the mountaintops exposed as if they're resting on clouds and not connected at all to the same earth as us. There are narrow waterfalls, gothic rock formations, terraced rice paddies, and forest canopy as far as I can see. We hear thunder some days that isn't really thunder but bombing raids over the horizon on other sections of the network of trails. Twice at night the sky blazes with lightning that isn't lightning, either, and more thunder. We see gashes in the jungle where jets have been shot down, and crashed and burned; black napalm smears on mountainsides; ghost valleys bleached white by Agent Orange.

But for all that, there's still more jungle that will never be destroyed or burned or erased, still more hidden trails and paths and roads and supply stations and columns of bo doi making the anguished months-long trek, carrying the war through the Wild West of Laos and Cambodia down into South Vietnam.

The terrain gradually changes as we descend from the high

trails, until we find ourselves winding our way through groves of giant bamboo. Phuong says it means we're getting closer to Nong Fa. She says she was there once before, but she doesn't remember to warn us that the bamboo will be alive with ants. And that they will rain down on us as we brush the stalks and leave us bloody with their deep bites. We try going faster, but slapping at the ants, brushing them off as soon as they land, or trying to, makes that impossible. They're everywhere. In my hair, all over my face and arms, inside my clothes. I slap and dance and curse. We all do. But there's no escape except to keep going.

The forest floor is strewn with razor-sharp bamboo slivers that are another hazard, our sandals barely enough protection for the undersides of our feet, and no protection at all for the sides, or our ankles and calves. Every step brings more cuts, more ant bites, more misery. We leave a bloody trail and practically cry with relief when we finally emerge out of the bamboo nightmare and into pine forest, with soft needles cushioning the way forward.

We come to another village, with a circle of men drinking through long green bamboo straws from a metal container fashioned from a bomb casing. Phuong says they're Taliang people, and they're drinking fermented rice, something called lao hai. They grunt when we approach but wave us off when Phuong tries to negotiate with them for food. We leave empty-handed, though they do let us wash off our blood in a small stream that snakes through their compound, with a small footbridge connecting their huts and animal pens on each side. Khiem looks longingly at a fat boar and caresses his machete.

That afternoon, we come across an enormous python in the process of swallowing a barking deer. Only the forelegs and head are still visible. The deer is somehow alive, its eyes wide with silent panic, its tongue hanging out as it gasps for air. Phuong lets Khiem use his machete this time, and he puts the barking deer out of its misery. We take the front half; the python keeps the rest.

━━━━━━━━━━

A couple of hours later, after a sharp descent through the evergreen forest, we reach the rocky shore of Nong Fa, a clear blue bowl at least a mile across to more distant green hills—islands or peninsulas, it's impossible to tell. I sink to my knees in the face of it, the ridiculous beauty opening before us like a dream. Cloudless sky. Cool cross-breezes kissing the water, stirring up intersecting ripples. Phuong and Khiem sit on rocks next to me. We slip out of our sandals and slide our feet into the lake. It wouldn't surprise me if all my wounds are healed when I pull them back out.

"Are you going in?" I ask Phuong.

"The bottom is too soft for wading," she says. "So this may be as far in as I go. But you're welcome to swim—as long as you stay close to the shore."

She puts her sandals on, stands up, and studies the boundaries of the lake. I follow her gaze, picturing American gunships blasting over the horizon, swooping in low over the lake, while NVA commandos in camouflage burst from their hiding places with their antiaircraft weapons, Phuong and Khiem and me caught in the middle.

But the afternoon stays quiet.

Khiem leaves to gather firewood, so he can roast the barking deer. He didn't bother to dress the carcass before, but just slung it over his shoulder and carried it with us, blood and guts dripping behind him. Phuong follows him to help. I stay at the water's edge, with nowhere else to go, and try wading in. Like Phuong said, there's no solid bottom, though, just soft ground that gives way so that almost as soon as I start in, I'm up to my chin and treading water. Clouds of sediment rise around me like a dirty bath. I swim out to clear water, duck under, and scrub my face and hair clean of all the sweat and grime. Then I turn over and float on my back under the pale blue sky.

No gunships come into view. No bombs. No automatic weapon fire. No rescue attempt. No ambush.

March 24

We eat blackened deer. We rest. Khiem rouses himself, fashions a fishing line, and returns to the lake, to a rocky spot a hundred yards away from where we set up camp. Phuong cleans her weapon. I go back to the water's edge, swim again, sit some more until it gets too hot, then move into the shade. And wait for what's to come. Phuong cleans her AK a second time and keeps glancing around nervously. Twice she follows Khiem to his fishing spot and then disappears into the pine forest. She doesn't say anything when she returns about where she's been, but I have my suspicions. Hard as I try, though, I don't see any signs of the NVA commandos hiding out there, preparing for the ambush.

At dusk we eat Khiem's fish. He insists we finish it all and then dispose of the bones and scales and guts far from our campsite, because if there's any left, bears might come. Phuong translates.

That night, unable to sleep, I ask Phuong if she's still awake. We're lying on beds of soft pine needles, just inside the forest cover, which feels luxurious in contrast to the hard ground that we've slept on for weeks. I can see the lake, the distant hills, the stars. A chill wind blows over the water. The air is filled with the citrus scent of a thousand orchids growing on the trees.

She says yes, she's awake. She says she can't sleep, either. Anticipating. She doesn't say anticipating what, but she doesn't have to.

I want to ask her where she went during the day, and if she knows where the commandos are hiding, if she's been in touch with them. I want to ask if she was letting me swim alone, without her or Khiem close by standing guard, because that's part of the ambush plan.

But I know she won't answer any of those questions. So instead I ask something I think she will. "What will you do after the war, Phuong?"

It takes a long time for her to respond. "I will return home to my family, of course," she says. "I wouldn't want to let them out of my sight for a very long time. My brothers and sisters. My aunts and uncles and cousins. My grandparents. If they're still alive. They were already very old when I left Hanoi two years ago. I would want to eat everything my mother used to cook for me when I was a girl. Her pho bo rien, banh xeo pancakes, spring rolls, dragon fruit.

"If the bombing stopped, I would go for a long walk every day all around Hanoi—along the Red River, which the old people still call Ascending Dragon. Across Long Bien Bridge. Through the French Quarter, around Hoan Kiem Lake—the Lake of the Returned Sword—through Ba Dinh Square. I would take my little sisters to mountain gardens filled with sea flowers and daisy nightingale and milk flowers and lotus. We would visit the Buddhist pagodas, if they're still standing after the war, and pray for our ancestors, and for all who've been lost."

She sighs. "And I would go back to school," she says. "I've always loved being in school, and I've missed so many years already.

"To become a doctor," she adds. "There will be so many who need help after the war. So many injured and crippled. So many to be made whole again."

We're silent for a while. I've only been away from my home and family for two months, and I'm heartsick and homesick. For Phuong it's been two years. I can't imagine how difficult that must be.

"And what will you do after the war?" she asks.

"I don't know," I say. "Before I would have told you I'd go back home to New York, and go to concerts, and hang out with my best friend, Geoff. Go to the Hamptons to my grandparents' house and let them spoil me there. Go back to school. Just have fun. But now . . ." I trail off.

"Now the first thing I would do is make sure my parents are okay, and then I'd be nicer to them. My dad, he's such a big believer in the war. I wouldn't know what to say to him about it, except to ask him to please let somebody else take over so he can come home and we can be a family again, him and me and my mom. I would tell him that I've missed him, and I want him back."

I think hard about the question. After the war. After the war. My stomach growls. "And I would definitely eat, too," I add. "A lot. Pizza. For breakfast, lunch, and dinner I would eat pizza. And bagels and cream cheese. And hamburgers and french fries and chocolate milkshakes.

"But I don't know besides that. Being here. What we've seen and done since Saigon. It's just—the world isn't the same anymore. I don't know what my place is in it anymore. I don't know if I *have* a place anymore."

══════════════════

I wake up with sharp stomach cramps deep in the timelessness of night. I have to go to the bathroom—bad. I sit up suddenly. Khiem sits up, too. I point to my abdomen and make a face, hoping he can see me well enough in the shadows to understand. He nods and I plunge into the forest, wading through brush and ferns until I'm out of sight and can squat and do my business in privacy.

It doesn't take long, but I stay squatting for a few more minutes, just in case.

A soft breeze whispers through the pines. An owl or something like it flies over my head, so close I duck. I reach back to pull my pants up from down around my ankles, and then freeze, sensing or maybe hearing something behind me. I steel myself to turn and look, but before I can, a hand clamps over my mouth, scaring me so bad that I nearly fall back into what I just did. I feel a breath on the side of my face, and then a voice—an American voice!—practically inside my ear and pitched so low I can barely hear: "You know how to swim? Nod if you do. Don't speak."

I nod.

"Good. First light tomorrow, early as you can get away, you have to swim your tail off across the lake to the other side. Understand?"

I nod again. My heart is beating so fast and so loud that I'm afraid Khiem will hear.

"It's maybe a mile across. Sure you can do a mile?"

Another nod. I tell myself to breathe.

"Look for a signal from us when you're halfway. That'll tell you where to swim to. If the North Viets come after you, in a boat or something, we'll have them in our sights once you make it that far. Don't worry about what's behind you. Just keep going, fast as you can. If they start shooting at you when we're in range, we'll shoot back."

He lets me turn around to look at him. He has black grease-paint covering his face, night-vision goggles on his helmet, full camouflage, a handgun, a string of grenades, a KA-BAR knife.

I think he's going to say something encouraging, but instead his last words to me are, "Don't screw up. You'll get yourself killed and get us killed, too."

Then he vanishes.

I take several more deep breaths, press my hand over my chest, as if that will stop my heart from pounding, then return to the edge of the forest and Khiem and Phuong. Both are sitting up, staring into the dark after me. As soon as I come into view, they lie back down on their nests of pine needles.

I don't think I'll sleep any more tonight as I play the conversation with the American over and over in my mind. I should be able to swim a mile. I've done it a hundred times. But that was before Vietnam, before the past two months, before I lost so much weight that my ribs stick out. What if I can't make it? What if I drown? What if Khiem shoots me before I can get away?

What if I freeze in the morning, right there at the water's edge? What if I never get any closer to home than this side of Nong Fa? My heart is racing again—panic-attack racing. I gulp in air. My head is spinning. Maybe I cry out, or whimper, or something else pathetic.

I feel a hand on my arm, light and warm. It's Phuong.

She says, "You were making noises. I think you were having a bad dream." She gives me her canteen. "Here. Drink some. Maybe it will help."

I thank her. A few hours earlier we were talking about our lives after the war—Phuong in Hanoi, me back in New York. The earth has shifted since then, into a new orbit. Who knows what it will look like when the sun comes up.

March 25

We have our sticky rice in the morning but no fish. I don't know if I can hold anything down anyway. My hands shake—not a lot, but enough that twice I drop rice in the sand. Phuong asks if I'm all right and reaches over. For a second I think she's going to put her hand on my arm again, but instead she picks the rice out of the sand, blows on it, and hands it back. I eat it because what else am I going to do, even though I get grit in my teeth.

"Do you feel better?" Phuong asks. "You seemed feverish last night."

"I think I was just dehydrated," I say.

She hands me a canteen—Le Phu's this time, the one I've been carrying—and urges me to drink more. We have a polite conversation about nothing. The kind you have with someone when there are secrets you can't let them know about, and they have their secrets, too.

Khiem finishes his rice and goes into the forest to do his morning business. Phuong asks if I'll teach her how to swim.

"Now?" I ask, panicked.

"Well, no," she says. "Perhaps the first lesson could be in another place, where the water is shallow. They say Nong Fa has no bottom, so I think it would be too deep for me here, but I would like to learn one day. I've always wanted to swim in the ocean, especially at Tuan Chau Island. My parents took us there once, before the war, but we only waded in the surf."

"Were you on a vacation?" I ask, relieved that Phuong doesn't want me to teach her today.

She smiles. "I suppose we were. I don't remember ever going on a holiday before or after that. Maybe it was a special occasion. I was just a little girl. The ocean was so big, and I was terrified, but at the same time I wanted so badly to be out in it."

I promise I'll teach her when we're farther up the Trail, some-place where she can touch bottom.

"I would like that very much," she says. She cleaned her AK-47 twice the day before and has been cradling it in her lap while we talk. She begins breaking it down to clean it again.

It's time.

"I think I'll go for a swim now," I say, standing up. My legs are shaking. I pray she won't notice. I glance back at the forest, but there's no sign of Khiem yet.

Phuong smiles and nods. She tells me to be careful, then turns her attention back to the gun.

I look at the lake. I look across the water to the distant shore-line, which seems twice as far as it did the day before. I wonder what signal there will be—if I make it far enough for the commandos to even bother. I take a deep breath and let it out slow.

"Good-bye, Phuong," I say.

She smiles again. "Good-bye, Taylor."

Once again my feet sink into the filmy sediment as I step into the water, and I splash forward immediately. I swim out fifty yards, then lift my head, turn around and look back to shore. Khiem has returned. He's sitting next to Phuong and breaking down his weapon, too. I wave. Khiem doesn't respond, not that I expect him to. Phuong waves back. I wonder if she suspects what's about to happen.

I tread water for a little longer, keeping my gaze on her. I'm looking for something, but have no idea what. Maybe she's looking for something, too.

Then I take off, swimming freestyle, praying that I'll be strong enough and fast enough to make it to the other side.

Five minutes into the swim I pull off my clothes. They're so heavy, dragging so much, that it hardly seems as if I'm making any progress. I'm afraid Khiem will start shooting any second. I have to go faster. I pick up speed and swim hard for several minutes, just like old times in the pool with the swim team. It feels good to stretch out without the anchor of wet clothes. I might not have ever been fast, but I always had good form. I let myself glance back and sure enough, the shore has receded. Khiem and Phuong are standing now—I can see that much—and waving, maybe yelling, though I can't hear anything. Khiem raises his AK-47 and takes aim at me. Phuong pushes the barrel away, toward the ground.

I try to swim faster, keeping with freestyle for as long as I can, as far across the lake as it will take me, until fatigue sets in, then I switch to breaststroke, which makes it easier to study the far shore for whatever signal the commandos send. After another ten minutes in the water, I finally see it: a flash of light, like a hand mirror reflecting the morning sun. I swim toward the light.

I settle into a new pattern of ten strokes freestyle, ten strokes breast, back and forth, and when my arms lose all feeling and I think I can't go any farther, I kick backstroke, which is the closest I can come to resting. I know there's no way I can stop again.

The lake is flat, but I still manage to breathe in water, which sends me into a coughing fit. My chest feels like it's on fire. I get side cramps. Nausea. But I keep going. Backstroke kicking again. Breaststroke. I no longer have the strength for freestyle. My arms won't cooperate. My legs go dead. My breaststroke is more like dog-paddling. I see the mirror flash again, closer. Something zips through the water near me. It must be Khiem, Phuong no longer stopping him from shooting at me. I can't stop to look around, to find out. I dive underwater and swim as far as I can holding my breath—which isn't far at all. I try freestyle again. I flip over on my back again. I kick and kick and kick, but I keep going under, keep swallowing water, keep breathing it in and choking.

And then someone is with me in the lake—throwing an arm across my chest, gripping my side, pulling me against him, swimming for me, swimming for both of us. Other hands lift me, drag me onto land, drop me onto my back.

There are voices, but I'm blind, incoherent from all the lake water in my eyes, my nose, my mouth, my lungs.

"That him?"

"Yeah. Who else could it be?"

"Why's he naked?"

"Beats me. Guess he swam right out of his clothes."

"Somebody give him some shorts. That's embarrassing."

"No time. Grab him and let's go. Chopper will be at the LZ in five. Place has to be crawling with North Viets."

"Haven't seen any sign of them."

"Maybe not, but they're here, and we've gotta get out fast. No way they haven't figured out our position."

They half-carry, half-drag me through the forest and up a steep hill, threading our way around trees and bamboo stands, tearing through brush. I try to help, try to walk on my own, but they move too fast and I'm too weak. We burst into an open meadow just as a helicopter roars into view overhead and descends. The commandos crouch low to keep us clear of the whirling blades. The door gunner waves us in with one hand, keeping his other on his M60. We dash toward the chopper.

They throw me on board. They throw themselves in after me. They yell to the pilot, "Go, go, go, go, go!"

I feel the helicopter lift off the ground. And then the world explodes.

———————————————

Nearly everyone is hit by bullets or grenades or shrapnel. Something rips into my leg, and I bolt upright with a surge of adrenaline to see splintered bone and gristle. I reach down, to touch it, to make sure it's real, because that has to be somebody else's leg. No way it's mine. Someone falls on top of me. I can't push him off, but it doesn't matter because the pain, delayed by the shock, now sears my leg, my whole body, and all I can do is scream and scream and scream, only I'm not the only one scream- ing. Everybody is screaming: *Medic! Medic! Medic!* Bullets tear through the chopper as the pilot takes action, clipping the tops of trees, listing hard to one side, then overcorrecting to the other. The door gunner unloads everything he has, spraying bullets in every direction as I thrash around, crazy from the pain. Someone pulls the body off me, holds me down, pins my shoulders to the floor of the chopper. A medic ties a tourniquet above my knee, then stabs me with a syringe.

In minutes, the pain dulls and I'm in shock again, and trembling, dimly aware of the frantic activity going on all around me, wounded men helping one another with blankets and gauze and more syringes and more tourniquets, and the door gunner still firing at the jungle below as we pull farther away from the LZ and the ambush.

As if from a great distance I see the faces of the men who saved me, every one of them twisted in anguish and dripping with their own blood or the blood of their friends. I want to thank them and to apologize for swimming so slow, for getting them into this mess, but I've lost the power of speech.

═══════════════════════

There are two miracles that day.

The first miracle is that the helicopter, which by all the laws of physics should be destroyed under the furious onslaught of automatic weapons fire, is still able to lift off and make its way thirty miles to a firebase with a field hospital in the foothills of the Truong Son mountains, back in Vietnam.

The second is that—though no one on board will ever be whole again—everyone lives.

March 25, evening

Dad is waiting at the firebase when the rescue chopper lands, and he helps carry my stretcher to the field hospital. I've never seen him cry before, not even when his own dad died, but in my morphine haze I'm dimly aware that his eyes are rimmed with tears as they rush me into surgery. He stays in the tent as the field surgeon works furiously to staunch the bleeding from my leg wound. Nurses give me transfusions to replace all the blood I've lost. They cover me with a clean blanket.

I'm conscious, though just barely so, coming out of anesthesia, when the surgeon speaks to Dad. "I'm sorry, Major Sorenson," he says. "It doesn't look as if we'll be able to save his leg."

Dad curses, loud, and then orders the surgeon to do more. "That is not acceptable," he says, in his sternest voice, the one that always scared me when I was little. "My son will not lose his leg. It's not an option."

The surgeon says he'll do what he can, but Dad interrupts and says he expects hourly reports on my condition, and a detailed plan by tomorrow morning for how they'll save my leg. End of story. It's almost as if he's talking about something else besides me and the leg that I might lose. But of course I won't lose it, because nobody ever wants to disappoint my dad.

The surgeon stammers that he'll take care of everything, then makes his escape. Dad turns his attention to me. "Hey, sport," he says. "How you doing?"

My throat is too dry for me to speak. My tongue swollen. He lifts my head and tilts a cup of water to my lips. It hurts to swallow, but I drink it all. The first thing I manage to say is, "My leg?"

Dad frowns. "Going to need more surgery, I won't kid you. You're going to pull through."

"But will I lose it?" I ask. "I heard what they said. Are they going to have to amputate?"

He doesn't answer right away and my heart sinks. I start to cry.

"Hey, hey," he says. "Nobody's taking off your leg. I promise. I won't let them. You're going to be okay."

I sink back into unconsciousness. This goes on for the next couple of days. Waking up, asking about my leg, fading out. Dad is always there, though, and I know nothing bad can happen to me now. He'll take care of me. He'll make sure I keep my leg.

When I can stay conscious for more than five minutes, Dad asks me what happened the night of Tet. I tell him as much as I can remember about Hanh and Bunny Bunny Go Go, about the murdered MPs in Cholon, about TJ and the underground hospital, about the tunnels where I was interrogated, about the American commandos in the bamboo cage, about the elephant, about the bear, about the bombies and the kids, about Vu and Trang and Le Phu and Khiem, about the Lake in the Sky, about the Trail. About Phuong.

Dad unleashes a long string of curse words about Hanh and everything he's going to make sure happens to him once he's caught.

I'm staring at him, wide-eyed, wondering if that's what this is all about—Dad being more worked up about Hanh than he is about me? But that can't be.

He stops his tirade abruptly and once again turns his attention back to me. "I'm sorry, son," he says. "I'm so sorry. It's just that your mother and I were afraid we'd lost you. I know she blames me for what happened to you and thinks it was my fault. And I don't know that she's wrong about that."

"It wasn't your fault, Dad," I say. "I was the one who ran off. I didn't know what would happen. I'm the one who's sorry, for you and Mom, for making you worry so much. I thought I'd never see you again. I thought they'd put me in the Hanoi Hilton and torture me."

I break down. "I just want to go home, Dad. Please can you just take me home? And you come home with me and Mom? Please?"

He puts his hand on my head and brushes the hair out of my face. "I'll try, Taylor. I promise I will."

But that's not what I want to hear. I'm done with the war. I need him to quit it, too.

━━━━━━━━━━━━━

Back in Saigon a few days later, once I'm stable enough for them to transfer me to the base hospital there, Mom fusses over me nonstop. She can't seem to stop hugging me and crying and telling me how much better everything's going to be now, just you wait and see. "It's our chance to start over," she says. "I haven't been a good mother. I know that now. You deserve so much better, and I'll make sure that I am the mother you deserve."

"No, Mom," I say. "It's not like that. I'm the one who screwed up. You didn't do anything."

But she insists. "Nonsense. You've always been a good boy." And now I know she's making things up. Or just deciding to forget the past. Or something. Not that I care. I was afraid everybody would be mad at me. I was afraid everything would have changed so much that nothing and no one would be familiar anymore. I was afraid I'd never get to see Mom and Dad again, never get to go home.

I ask Mom to tell me what happened to them the night of Tet. She doesn't want to say at first, but eventually I get it out of her. She says some of the embassy guards were killed protecting her and the others when the NVA attacked. She says the fighting in Saigon went on for several days, mostly in Cholon, where I was kidnapped. The NVA and Viet Cong held out there the longest. Thousands were killed. I guess they destroyed Cholon in order to save it, too.

She says she hasn't forgiven Dad, and she's not sure she ever will.

"Forgiven him for what?" I ask, though I tire quickly and can feel myself sinking into my bed, my brain going fuzzy.

"For being here," she says, as if that explains anything. "For us having to come here to be with him. For everything that happened to you."

"It's not his fault," I mutter, though maybe it is, but I'm fading out again and I'm not sure the words come out clearly enough for her to hear me. I don't know if it will make any difference even if she does.

Mom insists on a chartered jet to bring me back to New York. The best hospitals, she says. The finest doctors. The top surgeons.

"What about Dad?" I ask. "Is he coming, too?"

"Maybe," she says. "We'll see."

It takes another week to arrange, and by the time we get back to the States I've developed an infection in my leg. I'm flush with fever, hardly aware of anything, forced into ice baths when my temperature spikes, heavily sedated with painkillers. The New York doctors do everything they can—operation after operation, antibiotic cocktails, a river of morphine—but in the end have to amputate. I'm beyond caring by then. I just want my life back— that's what I tell myself, anyway, when I'm lucid enough—though even in my delirium I know that isn't going to happen.

When I wake up, my leg is gone. The stump is just above where my knee used to be, flaps of skin they saved sewn together to close the wound and provide some padding over the end. There doesn't seem to be anything they can do about the phantom pain, coming from parts of my leg and foot that don't exist anymore, that are just ashes in a hospital incinerator somewhere. But it hurts so bad down there that I beg for more morphine, anything to make the pain go away.

Mom keeps telling me everything will be all right. She says they'll fit me with a prosthesis, and nobody will be able to tell from a distance if I just wear pants, that I'll have a slight limp, that's all, but I can't hear any of that. I cover my face with the crook of my arm. Nothing will ever be okay again.

I don't know how Geoff finds out I'm back in the States, but he sneaks into intensive care one night to see me, a week after they take my leg. I wake up to his whispered voice, calling me up from the deep recesses of whatever medication they have me on.

I start crying before I even open my eyes. He's crying, too.

"Man, I was afraid you were dead," he says. "We heard all kinds of crazy stuff."

"I was," I answer, which doesn't make sense. Or maybe it does. That kid Taylor Sorenson—maybe he did die in Vietnam. Maybe I've come back as somebody else.

I try to say that to Geoff, but it doesn't come out right. I try harder but can tell that I'm being incoherent.

"It's okay, Taylor," he says. "We can talk another time. You can tell me everything then. You want me to just sit here with you for a while? I've missed you something terrible."

I nod. I've missed him something terrible, too.

April 22

Mom still blames Dad for everything that happened—for my being kidnapped and spirited away on the Ho Chi Minh Trail, for all the trauma, for me getting shot in the rescue, for losing my leg. I know none of it is his fault, not directly, anyway, and keep telling her that, but she won't listen. "I'm leaving him," she says. "He can stay in Vietnam until they drop an atomic bomb for all I care. I'm through. *We're* through."

Dad follows us home and gets a room in a hotel near the hospital. He times his visits for whenever Mom isn't here and around his frequent trips down to Washington for meetings at the Pentagon. I guess he's killing two birds with one stone—looking after both me and the war at the same time. We don't talk about what's going on with him and Mom. He doesn't bring it up, and I don't ask.

"I'm here for you, buddy" is all he says. "The only thing that's important right now is getting you back on your feet."

"You mean foot, don't you?" I say, but he scowls, not liking the joke.

"There's nothing you can't do with one good leg," he says. "Don't let anybody tell you different. I've seen plenty of good men come out of Veterans Administration hospitals in a lot worse shape than you. Some give up. The best ones refuse to let it stop them."

I want to yell at him that I bet plenty of those guys do give up, even if they're "the best"—and how can Dad know what's going on inside of anybody who's just lost their leg?

But I'm too tired, and it would make him mad, and it's just not worth the effort.

Dad goes with me to rehab, pushing me harder than the therapists. It's like I'm in boot camp and he's the drill instructor. If I cry from the pain, or out of frustration, or because I'm feeling sorry for myself, he tells me I have to knock it off, that I'm never going to get my strength back if I don't keep trying, and crying isn't trying.

My leg has to heal more before I can get a prosthesis, but in the meantime they want me up on crutches and building upper body strength to be ready. I hate every minute of the exercises, but Dad won't let me skip a single session.

"You just have to buck up," he says. Over and over. "You just have to buck up."

So I buck up, even through continuing bouts of phantom pain—and real pain, too, when I stumble and crash into things, which is a lot. I can tell he's proud of me for sticking to it. But I also suspect that once the project is over—my rehabilitation—he might not have the patience to stay. His trips down to DC get more frequent, sometimes two or three times a week. Mom still comes. Geoff comes, too, though he also tries to time his visits for when she's not around.

One night, after a particularly grueling day of physical therapy, I'm lying in bed, bathed in sweat, when Geoff comes in. "Quick shower and then we're out of here," he says. "You got some pants around here you can wear?"

"I'm not going anywhere," I say. "I'm too tired. Plus I haven't left the hospital since I got here."

"Oh, come on," he insists. "You remember those girls we were with that night at the Moby Grape concert? They're waiting for us in my car. They want to see you. Especially the one you hooked up with that night, Beth. Remember her? 'Cause she sure remembers you."

"No way," I say. "I'm not ready." The idea of Beth, of anybody, seeing me like I am, makes me so anxious that it's all I can do to keep from yelling at Geoff and kicking him out of my room.

But he won't take no for an answer and somehow wears down my resistance. And the next thing I know we're on an elevator heading down to the parking garage.

"Relax, man," Geoff says. "You're, like, a cult figure at Dalton. You're the Kid Who Got Kidnapped in Vietnam."

"Not funny," I say.

What I am, as it turns out, is a freak show. Things start off okay with the girls, but pretty soon all I can think is that they're staring at what's no longer there, just an empty leg of my pants hanging there, useless, not even pinned up or anything, and Beth and Cassandra, the other girl, are doing everything except ask me about it, or about what happened in Vietnam. It's like when somebody has a blemish or scar or deformity on their face. People try to look anywhere but at the person's face, which only makes it that much more obvious what's on their minds. And pretty soon it's clear that it's the only thing on their minds.

The truth is that Beth and Cassandra can't be nicer. But that's part of the problem, too. They're working so hard to be nice that nothing's natural. And I feel tongue-tied and awkward and self-conscious about not just my leg, but about how emaciated I must look to them, about how tight I have to cinch my belt to hold my jeans up, about how pasty I am from all this time in the hospital, and my ragged hair. I'm self-conscious about how little I have to say to anybody. How little of me is left. Finally I tell them I have to go, that I have an early rehab session in the morning, which isn't true.

"Will we see you again?" Beth asks.

I hesitate for a second before answering: "No, I don't think so." It's about the only honest thing I say all evening.

———————————————

They fit me with my prosthesis a week later, but it takes a long time to learn to walk on it without falling on my face. Once I get the hang of it, though, Dad tells me he has to go back to Vietnam. "I'll come home again," he says. "As soon as things are stable over there. Sooner. I promise."

But we all know it's a war of broken promises. And I must have known all along, deep inside, anyway, that Dad being here with me was only temporary.

There's one thing I have to ask him before he leaves. I know he's going to get mad, but I have to know.

"Dad," I say on his last day. "What you do in Vietnam. Your job. The people who kidnapped me said you were CIA."

"People say a lot of things," he says.

"So are you? And they also said you're one of the Architects—that that's what they call you and the others."

"What others?" he asks. "What architects? Not sure what you're talking about, Taylor."

"The Trail," I say. "The Ho Chi Minh Trail. The Reunification

Trail. Blood Road. They said you're responsible for planning the bombings, the land mines, the bouncing bombs. And Agent Orange. The commando raids. Even stuff like seeding clouds to make it rain more and mess up the trails."

Dad doesn't get angry and I'm relieved. He just shrugs. "Like I told you, people say a lot of things. What you're describing, that's the war, son. Things happen in war. Things have to be done. Tough decisions have to be made. There's always a cost."

"I saw little kids, Dad," I say. "Bodies. Burnt. In pieces." I can't seem to get out what I want to say. If I try to describe what I've seen, I know I'll start crying again, and Dad hates it when I cry.

"Look," he says, "you didn't question me like this about the Second World War. You know I fought in that war. You know I was responsible for people who died in that war. Because I shot them or ordered my men to shoot them or when I called in air strikes and artillery. I was responsible for the loss of a lot of lives on our side, too, good men I ordered into battle who didn't survive. That's just something I had to live with. People die in war."

"I know, Dad," I say. "I know you did what you had to do."

"Do you know how many people died in that war?" he asks.

I shake my head.

"Eighty million, that's how many. Give or take ten million or so. It's impossible to know exactly." He pauses to let that sink in, then he says, "And do you know how many of them were civilians?"

He doesn't wait for me to answer. "Sixty million. Three out of every four who died in World War II were civilians. And do you know what? It's always been that way. And when they add up all the casualties in Vietnam, it's going to be the same there."

"It's always been that way," I repeat. "That's the only explanation for what I saw over there? Dad, I carried body parts out of a hospital. Arms and legs and heads and torsos, torn up every way bodies can be torn up. Bodies burned so bad they were just skeletons and dust. And those kids who died. What did they ever do to anybody?"

Dad stares up at the ceiling. I can tell he's getting mad now. He doesn't want to have this conversation. He's exasperated with me. He thinks I'm soft. Despite everything I went through, everything I survived, everything I just told him, or tried to tell him, everything I witnessed.

"One day you'll understand," Dad says, and that's the end of it.

He flies back to Saigon the next day. I'm heartbroken again, because how many times and in how many ways can you lose your dad?

May 20

Mom and I move into the guest cottage in the Hamptons at my grandparents' estate. They're never home—always off on cathedral tours, European river cruises, spa weeks, their villa in Tuscany. Mom gives away her furs and jewelry and enrolls in nursing classes.

"I prayed every day back in Saigon that God would keep you safe," she tells me the night we move in. "I prayed that He would deliver you back to me, and if He did I promised I would devote my life to service for others."

She tells me that one day she was sitting on the veranda at Dad's compound, and she had what she called a "vastation." Bathed in heavenly light. Angel choir. Stuff like that. She was sure it was God answering her prayers, sealing the deal. A week later, I was rescued.

So she has to make good on her part of the bargain.

"What about Dad?" I ask.

"What about him?"

"Did you pray about him? I mean, was there any divine guidance or whatever for you and him, staying together or getting divorced and all that?"

"Not exactly," Mom says, not catching on that I'm joking. Or at best just maybe half-serious. "I just felt that if your father was going to continue the course he's on, it wouldn't fit with the new direction I'm supposed to take in my life. And it's not right for you, either. You need a father who will be here, and not a father who keeps choosing the war over his family."

I've never heard Mom talk like this. I'm not sure I've ever had a conversation with her that involved much thought about, well, anything, except how it related to her. This new Mom is going to take some getting used to.

━━━━━━━━━━━━━━━━━━━

Geoff drives out every other weekend, and he and Mom actually get along with each other. On his third time down, I'm sitting on the veranda, not doing anything, when he throws a pair of swimming trunks in my lap. "Found these in your bedroom," he says.

I hold them up with two fingers, then fling them back at him. "So?"

He tosses them at me again. "So we're going swimming," he says. "Gotta get you in shape for the swim team."

I shake my head. "Never going to happen." But he won't take no for an answer and bugs me until I agree to at least go in with him. It's a struggle wading through sand with my prosthesis, and by the time we get down to the water I'm dripping with sweat. I leave the prosthesis on the beach and lean on Geoff as I hop down to the ocean. We wade in together, but as soon as he lets me go, a wave knocks me down. More waves crash over me until I push off with my one leg and knife through the breakers to calmer water.

And the next thing I know, I'm swimming. I don't really need my flutter kick to stay afloat, though once I start my freestyle stroke I miss being able to do it. Geoff keeps close, in case I have trouble. He doesn't say that's why he's doing it, but I know.

The funny thing is that after all the physical therapy I did to build up my upper body strength, I can almost keep up with him, even just kicking with one leg. Geoff can't believe it.

After ten minutes swimming parallel to the shoreline, we head back in.

"Dude, we've definitely got to get you on the swim team again when you come back to school," Geoff says when we drag ourselves up onto dry land.

We're toweling off back on the beach, and I'm trying to figure out how to reattach my leg without getting sand inside the prosthesis.

"I kind of don't think I'll be going back," I say. "I'm planning to just do some night classes down here and get my GED."

"That's crazy," he says. "We have senior year coming up. We'll rule the school."

"I doubt that," I say. "And anyway, I don't really want to be a walking freak show, people staring and everything."

"That's just temporary," Geoff says. "People get used to anything. It's just because it's new and different. I hear girls dig guys with scars. They think you're tough or something."

"First, I don't think that's true. I think you made that up. And second, what I have isn't just a scar."

"So it's a war wound," he says. "That's even cooler, if you think about it."

I don't say anything else. I always thought Geoff knew so much more about everything than me, knew how to talk to girls, knew how to win arguments, knew how to get along with teachers, his parents, just about everybody, while still being true to what he believed. I still think that about him. But today, sitting here at the beach, having this conversation, I realize there's a gulf between us that we'll never be able to close, or even fully cross. He thinks this is about meeting girls and fitting in. But I'm still having flashbacks, waking up in the middle of the night, caught up in dreams about the MPs murdered right in front of me in Cholon; Trang blown apart by the land mine; Le Phu, her face destroyed by a bear; the little boy who lost his hands, and his life, playing with a bouncing bomb. I've been beaten and tortured and shot. I lost my leg. And I don't think I can say this to anybody, but I miss Phuong.

December 24

Today three astronauts orbited the moon. I guess it was just a matter of time. Next thing you know they'll have somebody landing on it, walking around, collecting rocks. Maybe they'll start a moon colony and if things get too bad on Earth, people will start moving in.

It's been a hard year.

Back in the spring, President Johnson announced he was halting the bombing of North Vietnam, and he wouldn't run for reelection.

Somebody assassinated Dr. Martin Luther King Jr. in Memphis, and it sparked riots all over America.

Bobby Kennedy was killed on the campaign trail. My mom always loved the Kennedys and was broken up about it for a long time.

Richard Nixon was elected president, which means the war isn't going to be ending anytime soon.

There were stories in the *New York Times* about destroyed

villages, burned crops, terrorized civilians, and inflated body counts in Vietnam. The chief of police in Saigon shot a captured Viet Cong spy in the head. Somebody took a picture the second the bullet struck. It was on the front page of all the newspapers.

The American commandos I met in the bamboo cage were officially declared MIA–Presumed Dead. Nobody wrote anything about that.

I've felt lost for the longest time, like I no longer speak the same language as the people around me. Sometimes I dream in French. I dream about Phuong and the Trail just about every night. The war in real life rages on; even with a halt to the bombing there's still no light at the end of the tunnel. I watch the nightly news, read the *Times*, check out books from the library on Vietnam. A few times back in the fall, I slipped out of the cottage at night and slept under a tree. The ground made more sense to me. Like I belonged there. Like I was back on the Trail. Mom begged me to tell her what's going on, but I couldn't talk about it—not with her, or with anybody, really. Even the therapist she insisted I see. After a couple of months Mom let me quit. The therapist told her our sessions weren't going anywhere, mostly because I just sat there silent.

I do talk about it some to Geoff, but only the bare outline. He doesn't push, and he hasn't abandoned me out of frustration because I won't open up. He just keeps coming to visit, to walk on the beach, to go for swims, no matter how cold the water is, to raid my grandparents' refrigerator and watch movies. Even with that gulf between us. And who knows, maybe it has shrunk a little.

I'm still embarrassed about my prosthesis. I hate when people notice me limping. I get tired of them asking what's wrong, and all the sympathy coloring their faces if I tell them. Geoff is so matter-of-fact about it, though, that eventually, over time, I've kind of learned to be matter-of-fact about it, too.

I didn't go back to Dalton. Instead I've been taking night classes in town and told Mom I don't want to go to college. Not just yet.

I've been looking hard to find some meaning to my life, buried in all I've been through, all I've seen, all the suffering and death I witnessed, and that I caused, however inadvertently. But I'm not having an easy time finding it. I go to church. I meditate. I listen to the new Beatles' double album with the all-white cover over and over. I volunteer at a school for refugee children, driven by that image I'll always have of the little boy who lost his hands and died in Phuong's lap.

While the astronauts return from orbiting the moon, I take a train into the city so the doctors can make adjustments to my prosthesis. It's been chafing for quite a while, and Mom finally noticed the bleeding. She asked why I hadn't said anything, and I said because I hadn't felt anything, which was only partly true.

Geoff meets me at the clinic. There are a lot of veterans here, as usual, missing legs, arms, hands, feet. He talks to a couple of them while I have my appointment. Afterward, heading back to Penn Station, he fills me in. "This one guy, he's in the Vietnam Veterans Against the War. He's been going to antiwar protests. And this other guy says he wishes he still had his arm, because he'd reenlist in a heartbeat and go back to Vietnam. They're still friends, though."

"That makes sense—after what they've been through, the politics of the war don't compare to how they feel about each other. Like brothers," I say.

Eventually I start limping from the long walk, so we stop at a sidewalk café so I can rest. The seats are freezing, but I barely notice.

"You think you'd ever go back?" Geoff asks. "I mean after the war, assuming it ever ends."

It takes me a long time to respond. At first I say, "I don't know," but then, after I think about it some more, I say, yeah, maybe I would. "And the war will definitely end," I add. "I mean, it might take twenty years, but North Vietnam will win. The trail soldiers will continue their supply missions, no matter how many cluster bombs and napalm drops and Dragon Ships and fighter-bombers and commando raids and spies and poisoned rice supplies we use against them. They'll sacrifice so much more than we ever will. Right or wrong, they're the ones who'll endure."

"Endure what?" Geoff asks.

"Anything," I say. "Everything. Literally everything."

"So that girl you were with over there," Geoff says, choosing his words carefully. "Phuong." This is new territory for us. "You don't hate her for keeping you prisoner all that time, and all the things they did to you—the beatings and the torture you told me about, and not knowing if your mom and dad were even alive, and all the rest of it? I mean, you lost your leg, man."

"She was just doing what she had to do," I say. "She was under orders. But she took care of me. Yeah, I saved her life, but I'm pretty sure she saved my life, too. I believe she told me what was going to happen at the lake because she *wanted* me to escape. I think she couldn't bear the thought of me in a Hanoi prison and all the things they'd do to me there."

Geoff shakes his head. "You think she's still alive? Think you'll ever see her again?"

"I can't imagine her not being alive," I say. "At least when I picture myself back in Vietnam, she's always there."

I pause before saying, "When the war ends and we have diplomatic relations or whatever, I was thinking, maybe I could go back there, to Hanoi, and find her. Maybe meet her family. Just, you know, go for a walk by the Red River, and all these famous places she told me about. Like, the French Quarter, and the Lake of the Returned Sword, and these mountain gardens they have there, and this island she told me about. She wanted me to teach her how to swim so she could go there again, so maybe I could do that."

Geoff nods. "You should take me with you. I think it'd be cool to see all that."

I say that'd be great, because I also have this other idea, though I don't mention that it just came to me, like a vastation of my own.

"Which is what?" Geoff asks.

"Which is Phuong and I learn how to disarm those cluster bombs. Get trained in how to do that. And we go back to the Trail, to find all the unexploded ones in Laos and Cambodia." I tell Geoff he can even come with us. It'll take a long time. There are millions of bombs. But we could be the ones who start. Because somebody has to do something.

"Sort of clean up the mess left by your dad?"

I nod. "Yeah. I guess something like that."

"You really think Phuong would help you with that?" Geoff asks.

"Maybe," I say. "At least we wouldn't be enemies anymore— not us and not Vietnam and America. We'd just be these two people who were together in the war. Who went through a lot. Just these two people who survived."

AUTHOR'S NOTE

While Taylor and Phuong's journey along the Ho Chi Minh Trail is fiction, the events leading up to it, including Taylor's trip to South Vietnam as a civilian, and what they experienced along the way are all based on historical events and accounts. The notorious Hanoi Hilton that Taylor fears is his destination was unfortunately a real prison where captured Americans were tortured in North Vietnam. The Vietnam War was a deeply complicated conflict that divided the US in a way nothing had since the Civil War, starting in 1961, when President Kennedy sent Green Berets and military advisers to train South Vietnamese troops, and continuing until January 1973, when the last US troops left—a long and tragic twelve years later.

Vietnamese rebels had already been fighting French colonial rule since before World War II, finally defeating French forces in the famous Battle of Dien Bien Phu in 1954. The victory by Ho Chi Minh's revolutionary army forced France out of Vietnam and led to the Geneva Accords, by which Vietnam was partitioned along the 17th parallel into communist-controlled North Vietnam, backed by China and the Soviet Union, and nominally democratic South Vietnam, supported—many would say controlled—by the United States.

The US began bombing North Vietnam and the Ho Chi Minh Trail in 1965 and sent the first US ground troops into South Vietnam that same year. The number of American troops in Vietnam grew quickly, from 185,000 in 1965 to a high of 535,000 three years later, fighting alongside nearly a million South Vietnamese troops in a war of attrition against the North Vietnamese Army and their Viet Cong guerrillas, who controlled hundreds of villages, towns, and even provinces throughout South Vietnam.

The Tet Offensive began on January 30, 1968, the start of the Vietnamese New Year, when 80,000 Viet Cong and North Vietnamese Army troops launched surprise attacks on more than one hundred South Vietnam towns and cities and military installations, including the capital, Saigon, where the attackers briefly overran the grounds of the US Embassy. The coordinated attacks came after the US government had assured the American public for months that the US and South Vietnam were winning the war, and that there was, in the words of then–Army Chief of Staff General William Westmoreland, "light at the end of the tunnel."

Though initially successful, the Tet Offensive ended in

military failure for the North Vietnamese Army, when all the captured cities and territory and installations were retaken in counterattacks by the US and South Vietnamese forces, who inflicted heavy casualties on the NVA. But the widely publicized attacks nonetheless shocked the American public, who had been led to believe that the enemy was too weak to mount any sort of massive and coordinated military campaign. With the rising number of American casualties, revelations of atrocities committed by some US soldiers, and mass protests against the war back home, support for the war fell in the aftermath of the Tet Offensive.

Support declined further when President Nixon ordered a resumption of the bombing in the North and in 1970 sent troops into Cambodia, widening the ground war at a time when an increasing number of Americans wanted it to end. Massive antiwar protests continued; the US began secret peace talks with the North; and in 1972, the NVA launched what was dubbed the Easter Offensive, once again attacking military bases throughout the South, and surprising the US and South Vietnamese forces. US troop levels, which also began a dramatic decline in the aftermath of the Tet Offensive, were down to 24,000 in 1972. The United States pulled the last of its troops from Vietnam a year later, in January 1973. The war ended in victory for the North Vietnamese two years after that when they defeated the South Vietnamese Army and entered Saigon on June 6, 1975.

The names of 58,307 Americans who died in the war are inscribed on the Vietnam Veterans Memorial in Washington, DC. Estimates of the total number of North and South Vietnamese, Laotians, and Cambodians killed in the war range from 1.5 million to 3.5 million, the majority of them civilians.

The US conducted nearly 600,000 bombing runs during the war and dropped more bombs on Vietnam, Cambodia, and Laos than had been dropped in all of World War II. Three million tons of those bombs—plus a near constant aerial spraying of chemical defoliants—were dropped on the 12,000 miles of roads, trails, and waterways that comprised what the North Vietnamese called the Truong Son Strategic Supply Route, and the Americans dubbed the Ho Chi Minh Trail. Hundreds of thousands of civilians and bo doi—NVA soldiers and trail workers—were killed or wounded in the bombings and spraying and clandestine assaults by US and South Vietnamese units. But the supply route, also called the Reunification Trail, or sometimes Blood Road, was never broken.

An estimated 80 million of 270 million cluster bombs dropped in Laos during the war—the baseball-size "bomblets" like the ones described in this story—remain in that impoverished country today, where hundreds of civilians still die every year from delayed explosions.

In the novel, Taylor Sorenson quotes his father as saying, "We had to destroy the village in order to save it." That quote, in slightly altered form, is borrowed from a February 7, 1968, dispatch by journalist Peter Arnett, writing about a small provincial capital in South Vietnam, and a US Army major's explanation for the decision to bomb the town to force out the Viet Cong, regardless of civilian casualties: "It became necessary to destroy the town to save it."

I am indebted to Virginia Morris and Clive Hills, who traveled the length of the Trail a decade ago, for their important contemporary study *A History of the Ho Chi Minh Trail: The Road to Freedom*, and to John Prados for his exhaustive political and historical account, *The Blood Road: The Ho Chi Minh Trail and the Vietnam War*. For insight into the lives of those who came down from North Vietnam to bring the fight to the South, I am deeply appreciative of Dang Thuy Tram's recently discovered wartime diary, published posthumously thirty years after she was killed in the war, *Last Night I Dreamed of Peace*. The *New York Times* Vietnam '67 series was enormously helpful, especially Ron Milam's essay "1967: The Era of Big Battles in Vietnam," and Hai Nguyen's "As the Earth Shook, They Stood Firm," both important accounts of the decimation of the village of Ben Suc. While I have relied on these and other sources to help ensure historical accuracy in *On Blood Road*, any mistakes are, of course, my own.

Acknowledgments

My deepest thanks, as always, to my agent, Kelly Sonnack; to my wife and partner, Janet Marshall Watkins; and to my editor, Jody Corbett, who's been as much coauthor as editor on this one. My thanks also to John Prados for his time and invaluable suggestions while this book was still in manuscript form, and to Professor Jim Gaines for his help with the French dialogue. And finally thanks to a host of terrific folks at Scholastic: Nina Goffi, Rachel Gluckstern, Jana Haussmann, and the rest of the sales, marketing, and publicity departments. Shakespeare said he hated ingratitude more "than lying, vainness, babbling, drunkenness, or any taint of vice whose strong corruption inhabits our frail blood." No worries about that here, as these folks will always have my deep and abiding gratitude for all their hard and talented work helping to bring *On Blood Road* into the world.

About the Author

Steve Watkins is the author of the novels *Juvie*; *What Comes After*; *Great Falls*; *Down Sand Mountain*, winner of the Golden Kite Award; *Sink or Swim*; and the Ghosts of War series, including *The Secret of Midway, Lost at Khe Sanh, AWOL in North Africa*, and *Fallen in Fredericksburg*.

A former professor of journalism, creative writing, and Vietnam War literature, Steve cofounded and helps a nonprofit yoga studio and works with an urban reforestation organization in his hometown of Fredericksburg, Virginia.